The Valley of
VANISHING HERDS

Center Point
Large Print

Also by W. C. Tuttle and available from
Center Point Large Print:

The Mystery of the Red Triangle

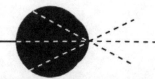

The Valley of
VANISHING HERDS

A Hashknife Hartley Story

W. C. TUTTLE

CENTER POINT LARGE PRINT
THORNDIKE, MAINE

This Center Point Large Print edition
is published in the year 2020 by arrangement with
Golden West Literary Agency.

Originally published in the US by Houghton Mifflin.

The text of this Large Print edition is unabridged.
In other aspects, this book may vary
from the original edition.
Printed in the United States of America
on permanent paper.
Set in 16-point Times New Roman type.

ISBN: 978-1-64358-612-0 (hardcover)
ISBN: 978-1-64358-616-8 (paperback)

The Library of Congress has cataloged this record under
Library of Congress Control Number: 2020930535

CONTENTS

CONTENTS

The Valley of
VANISHING HERDS

CHAPTER I

RED ANTS

IT WAS well after dark when the herd reached the old shipping corrals at Isabella. There was no breeze, and the dust-cloud, only a few feet from the ground, obscured them for a while as the weary cattle stopped. Cowboys swore quietly as they bunched the herd. The corral was far too small to hold the herd, and that meant night-herding.

They had ridden all day in the choking dust and heat, and they wanted to quench that thirst at the one saloon in Isabella and not have to take their turn in riding night herd. A fire glowed at the chuck-wagon, where the old range cook made supper.

Hashknife Hartley, gaunt, six feet four, his lean face grimy from dust and sweat, yanked off his saddle. Sleepy Stevens, his partner, rode in beside him and began unsaddling. No night-herding for them; they were through with the UF outfit and free to do as they pleased. That was the agreement when they came with the herd.

They moved over near the chuck-wagon, where several of the men had already gathered and were gently chiding the cook because supper was not quite ready. But the chuck-wagon cook is supreme in his own right and he paid them no attention.

Slim Sherrod, a tall buck-toothed cowboy, a newcomer to the UF, sprawled on a saddle-blanket smoking a cigarette. Dell Packer, the foreman of the outfit, rode in from the town and dismounted. Dell had the few pieces of mail for the boys. He handed the cook a letter and came over to Hashknife.

'Somebody in this outfit is important,' he laughed, as he handed Hashknife a telegram. 'Been here a week, they said.'

Everyone watched Hashknife as he read the telegram. Down there a telegram was usually bad news. Hashknife read it casually and handed it to Sleepy, who turned it toward the light of the fire in order to read it. Then he handed it back to Hashknife, without comment.

'Somebody died?' asked Slim.

'Prob'ly,' said Sleepy. 'They do it ever' once in a while.'

The telegram was from Bob Marsh, secretary of the Cattlemen's Association, and read:

AM ANXIOUS TO GET IN TOUCH WITH HENRY WEBSTER AT ANTE-LOPE FLATS. CAN YOU LOCATE HIM AND ASK HIM TO WRITE OR WIRE

ME AS IT IS VERY IMPORTANT.
REGARDS TO YOU AND SLEEPY.

It was a simple request, except that neither of
them had ever been at Antelope Flats, nor did
they know just where it was. The rest of the men
came hurrying in when the cook yelled 'Grub
pile!' and in a few moments the hungry cowboys
were too busy to talk.

Dell Packer came over and sat down beside
Hashknife to eat.

'Sorry yuh ain't goin' back with me,' he said.

'Thank yuh, Dell,' replied Hashknife. 'We like
the UF, but it ain't in us to stay long any place.'

'Yeah, I know,' nodded Dell. 'It's allus my
luck; when I get a puncher who knows how to
handle stock, he's also got a itchin' foot.'

'Have yuh ever been in Antelope Flats?' asked
Sleepy.

Dell shook his head. 'Never been up there,'
he said. 'It's up in Lost Horse Valley, about a
hundred and fifty miles from here.'

'Slim can tell yuh about it,' offered Shorty Hill.
'He's from up thataway.'

Slim Sherrod lifted his head and looked across
at Shorty.

'Who the hell told you all that?' he asked
quickly.

'Well, yuh wasn't talkin' in yore sleep, Slim,'
retorted Shorty.

'Anythin' wrong in bein' from there?' asked Dell curiously.

Slim laughed shortly and shook his head. 'Not a thing, Dell.'

'When you was up there, Slim,' said Hash-knife, 'did you ever know a man named Henry Webster?'

Slim scowled thoughtfully. 'Henry Webster? No, I never heard of one.'

'I knowed a feller named Webster,' said Shorty.

'Henry?' asked Sleepy.

'Nope—Daniel. He wrote a book. Wasn't very interestin', because he skipped from one thing to another too often.'

'What about this Webster at Antelope Flats?' asked Sherrod.

'I just thought maybe you knew him, Slim,' replied Hashknife.

'Well, I told yuh I didn't.'

'Then don't worry about him,' said Hashknife quietly.

'I ain't worryin'. Why'd yuh think I was worryin'?'

'If you ain't,' remarked Shorty, 'yo're showin' a hell of a lot of interest in a man yuh never knowed.'

'Drop it,' growled Les Hart, who bunked with Slim.

'That's what I say,' agreed Dell, tossing his plate aside. 'Slim, you and Les take the early shift. Want to walk over and see the town, Hashknife? It's sure a metropolis.'

The town of Isabella was a shipping point for all the cattle outfits in that part of the country, but it was still a one-horse cow-town, with one street, one big saloon, and possibly two dozen weatherbeaten houses. The depot was a quarter of a mile from the town.

There seemed to be some commotion in the saloon as the group of men from the UF spread came up on the porch. There were possibly two dozen men in the place, and their interest was centered on a young man at the bar. This particular young man was attired in a flaming red shirt, the gaudiest pair of chaps ever seen in that vicinity, an expensive white Stetson, and patent-leather, high-heel boots.

He was a very mild-looking young man, wearing horn-rimmed glasses, and his complexion showed clearly that very little Arizona sun had ever got a chance at his skin. At the end of the bar was a skinny little rawhider, also wearing an expensive Stetson, which was a trifle too large, and which kept sliding down over his eyes. His legs were as bowed as a barrel-hoop.

Facing the young man was a big, rough product of the cow-country, grim and hairy, a heavy gun swinging at his thigh, a shapeless sombrero yanked down over one eye. Evidently they had been having words as Hashknife and the rest of the boys came in.

The hairy one said: 'Yo're a hell of a specimen, feller. If you talk back to me, I'll squirsh yuh, jist like I would a fancy bug.'

The audience chuckled, but it did not seem funny to the young man.

'There is no such word as "squirsh," ' he said.

'You tryin' to tell me how to talk?' snarled the cowboy.

'The correct use of English, my dear man—'

'English!' snorted the cowboy. 'I'm United States—and I talk like I damn please, you pink-faced dude!'

The young man's brows lifted slightly and he looked around at the faces partly obscured in the tobacco smoke.

'Artemus,' he said quietly.

The little bowlegged rawhider cuffed the hat away from his eyes, shrunk a little as he said, 'Yessir.'

'I believe we will go now, Artemus.'

'I tried to tell yuh fifteen minutes ago that the train had done left,' complained Artemus.

'Artemus!' snorted the hairy one. 'My Gawd!'

Artemus let the hat slide down over his eyes again. The hairy one moved over close to the young man, his jaw sticking out belligerently.

'You ain't goin' no place, Handsome,' he snarled. 'When I git through—'

14

Whap! The innocent-looking young man suddenly uppercut with his left hand, connected solidly with the hairy one's chin, and the belligerent cowboy went down like a poleaxed steer. Then the young man reached down, yanked the cowboy's gun from his holster, turned to face the stunned audience, and started backing toward the doorway, the gun wavering in his hand.

'Come, Artemus,' he said.

The little rawhider had his big hat in his hand now, staring at the young man. The room was still.

Artemus said in a strained voice: 'I'll be a dry-nurse to a dinny-sour—I shore will!'

The young man was still backing toward the doorway, where he backed into a chair, fell over it, and landed on the floor, the gun flying out of his hand. Artemus stopped and looked around. The young man sat up and shook his head.

'I cannot seem to do anything right,' he said quietly.

The hairy one was on his knees, shaking his head. He saw the gun and made a dive at it, but Hashknife kicked it away from his clawing hand.

'Thank you kindly,' said the young man, looking up at Hashknife, his glasses slightly askew. 'That man is ignorant enough to shoot one.'

Then he got to his feet and walked out, followed by Artemus, who flinched as though expecting

15

a kick from the rear. The crowd, all except the hairy one, howled. The hairy one had lost a front tooth.

'Did yuh ever see a pair like that, Hashknife?' asked Dell.

Hashknife shook his head.

The hairy one said, 'I'm goin' t' find him and beat him to death.'

'He'd do it, too,' confided Dell. 'That's Buck Shell. If I was that tenderfoot, I'd hide out tonight.'

While the crowd was talking things over, Hashknife and Sleepy left the saloon and went to the hotel, where they found the two men talking with the proprietor about a suite of rooms, with baths.

'We ain't got no sweets and I never heard of none,' said the proprietor. 'And you'll have to git yore bath at the barber shop. We just sell rooms and a bed.'

The young man saw Hashknife and smiled. Artemus adjusted his hat and leaned against the counter. Hashknife and Sleepy sat down and the young man joined them.

'I am grateful to you,' he told Hashknife. 'That detestable person might have fired that gun at me.'

'Yeah, and you better look out for that detestable person,' said Hashknife. 'He is Buck Shell.'

Artemus came over and sat down, slightly ill at ease. He grinned at Sleepy. The name did not fit Artemus.

The young man said, 'I am Alexander Hamilton Montgomery.'

'Sounds like the Civil War had met a mail-order house,' said Sleepy.

'And this man,' continued the young man, 'is Artemus Day, my valet.'

'Mostly I'm called Smoky,' said Artemus.

'A valet?' queried Hashknife.

'Whatever that is,' nodded Artemus. 'I'm learnin' him the West.'

'I engaged him in Cheyenne,' informed Montgomery.

'I was drunk,' said Artemus.

'That is his failing,' sighed Montgomery. 'Liquor and poker.'

'I handle liquor better'n I do poker,' admitted Artemus. 'Give me a pair of deuces and I become poverty-stricken immediate. I had a royal flush oncet and'—Artemus gazed dreamily at the ceiling—'it was a credit game, with a two-bit limit.'

'Looking back at the incident this evening,' said Montgomery, 'you were of no assistance to me, Artemus.'

'Well,' replied Artemus, 'you've told me lots of times that if you wanted me for anythin', you'd call me.'

'But under such circumstances I believe you should come to my assistance without being asked. After all, you are my valet.'

'Uh-huh,' said Artemus. 'I s'pose yo're right—but yuh didn't need me.'

'Would you have come had I needed you?'

'Uh-huh. I ain't never backed down yet. I told yuh I'd learn yuh all about the West, and I meant it. That there hairy jasper that yuh whangdoodled with a left uppercut is a plumb salty *hombre*. He'd shoot yuh jist to see yuh kick.'

'Kick?' queried Montgomery. 'Dead men don't kick—or do they?'

'Not after a certain len'th of time. But yuh don't have to die ever' time yuh get shot. At least, I never did.'

'Have you been shot, Artemus?' queried Montgomery.

'Times too numerous t' mention. One time I took on seven men, single-handed. They all had shotguns, and all I had was a pick-handle. Man, when they picked me up I rattled like a handful of poker-chips. The sheriff said, "Easy boys, or he'll plumb tear in two." Then they sewed me together with a sack-needle and bindin'-twine, and inside two weeks I was back ridin' broncs. And you wonder if I'd back yore play! Say, the only reason I didn't go right in and 'nihilate that *pelicano* was because I hate to take on less'n three at a time.'

'My goodness!' exclaimed Montgomery. 'But wh-what happened to the seven men, Artemus?'

Artemus snapped his fingers and gestured indifferently.

'You mean—you killed them, Artemus?'

'For a tenderfoot, you sure have a understandin',' replied Artemus.

Sleepy's face was red from suppressed laughter, and Hashknife was having a difficult time in concealing his mirth. A young man in a cowtown, with a valet!

Hashknife controlled his emotions and asked, 'Mr. Montgomery, just what are you doing in Isabella?'

'We got left,' said Artemus. 'Train had a hotbox, so we came over here to see what the place looked like.'

'Oh, you were just passin' through, eh?' queried Sleepy.

'Exactly,' nodded Montgomery. 'I am studying the West. I am a playwright. At least, I feel that I am. I also feel that the great drama of the West has never been written. That is my mission, Mr.—er—'

'My name is Hartley,' smiled Hashknife. 'Hashknife Hartley. This gentleman is Sleepy Stevens.'

Artemus was staring at Hashknife, his jaw sagging. He said: 'Hashknife Hartley? I'll be a dry-nurse to a dinny-sour!'

'What is wrong with you, Artemus?' asked Montgomery.

'Nothin',' replied Artemus. 'Jist a—a funny name, thassall.'

'I must put that name in my notebook,' said Montgomery. 'Now, where did I put that book? Did I leave it on the train?'

'Mebbe,' nodded Artemus. 'I—I'll remember it for yuh.'

A man came from the rear of the hotel. He was a tall, severe-looking man, carrying a heavy cane. He said to Montgomery: 'There's another train through here in an hour, and I wish you'd take it. I'll see that yuh get there safely. I'm the marshal of Isabella.'

'You ain't aimin' to run us out, are yuh?' asked Artemus.

'I reckon you can walk. Fact of the matter is, Buck Shell and his gang are gettin' drunk. When they're drunk, they're bad enough to handle without you around to make it worse. I don't want anybody to get killed and I don't want to have to kill anybody. I hope you see my point of view.'

'Oh, sure,' nodded Artemus.

Montgomery turned to Hashknife. 'If you were in my place, would you go?' he asked soberly.

'If I were in yore place,' replied Hashknife, 'I would have been holed up under that depot platform an hour ago.'

'Thank you very much. Officer, we are ready. Come, Artemus.'

'Shore glad to meetcha,' said Artemus.

'Where are you headin' for?' asked Sleepy.

'Antelope Flats,' replied Artemus. 'I ain't been there for a long time. Dang 'em, they said I'd never amount to anythin'. You wait'll they see me. No forty-a-month cowpunchin' for me. I'll high-tone that bunch.'

'Good luck to yuh, Mr. Montgomery,' said Hashknife.

'Thank you very much, sir.'

The three men walked out, and Sleepy doubled over in his chair.

'I'm glad they're gone,' he said huskily. 'A man can't stand much of that kinda stuff. Artemus! That little bowlegged sidewinder—Artemus! What's a playwright, Hashknife?'

'Writes theater plays, I reckon.'

'My Gawd, I wonder where he got the clothes!'

'Who knows? I'll bet he bought that hat for Artemus. No puncher ever had money enough to buy that kind of a hat. And they're goin' to Antelope Flats. That's where Henry Webster lives. Maybe we'll see 'em again. Let's go back to the wagon and get some sleep.'

Slim Sherrod and Les Hart were at the wagon getting some coffee when Hashknife and Sleepy came back. They had about two more hours to ride the herd before another relief would take their places. Hashknife and Sleepy spread their bed-rolls between the wagon and the corral fence and were crawling into their blankets when the two riders went away.

But Hashknife and Sleepy were only in their bed-rolls about five minutes when they went right away from there. Red ants! Millions of them!

They shook out their bedding, went a hundred feet away from that spot, and lighted matches to examine the ground before going to bed again. Tony Cano and Shorty Hill came back from town, well filled with Isabella whiskey, and their arguments awakened Hashknife and Sleepy.

'Watch 'em!' chuckled Sleepy. 'They're bunkin' down right on top of our anthill.'

'They're so full of bad liquor that even an ant wouldn't bite 'em,' replied Hashknife.

The two men stretched out in their blankets, and even at a hundred feet their snores could be heard.

After a while Sleepy said, 'Yeah, I reckon they're ant-proof.'

They were nearly asleep again when the report of a gun, only a short distance away, brought them upright in their blankets. It was like a clap of thunder. A man yelled painfully and was threshing around on the ground.

'What happened?' yelled Sleepy.

'I'm shot!' howled Shorty Hill. 'Somebody shot me! Get a doctor, I'm dyin'!'

'He's sober enough to realize death,' said Sleepy.

Shorty was out of his blankets, pawing at himself and staggering around. The cook came running, trailing a blanket over one shoulder and carrying an unlighted lantern, which he was holding high. Sleepy lighted it.

'If yo're dyin', why don'tcha lay down?' asked the cook.

'The bullet went the whole len'th of me!' wailed Shorty. 'Right into one end and out the other. I felt her go all the way.'

'Hold still while I look yuh over,' ordered Hashknife.

Shorty stood there, swaying like a sapling in a breeze, his face white in the lantern light. The bullet had cut through a fold of his undershirt, left a red furrow above his knee, and gone out through the foot of his bed-roll.

'You ain't hurt,' said Hashknife.

'I ain't?' asked Shorty, greatly relieved. 'I thought I was dyin'.'

'The Isabella whiskey was dyin', that's all,' said the cook. 'Have you got any enemies down here, Shorty?'

'I ain't got none no place,' declared Shorty. 'Git that lantern away from me! Lightin' me up that-away! Mebbe he's out there in the dark, notchin' a sight on me—and yo're helpin' him.'

'You ain't got no past, have yuh?' asked the cook.

'No, and I won't have no future if yuh don't quit makin' a target out of me. That's the first time I ever got shot.'

'You ain't been shot yet,' growled the cook. 'You was missed.'

'What about that red mark on my laig?' demanded Shorty. 'Ants don't have plows. Look at the end of my bed-roll. Look at my shirt. Don't tell me that an ant done that. I've been shot at.'

'Mebbe,' the cook suggested, 'Buck Shell thought you was the tenderfoot.'

'Aw-w-w, Gawd, I don't look like that thing.'

'Go to sleep—yo're all right,' advised the cook.

'Sleep? Me? I'm goin' to set up all night with a gun in my hand. Nobody ever can say that Shorty Hill died without a struggle.'

'I don't think he'll come back,' said Hashknife.

'Thinkin',' said Shorty, 'ain't goin' to do me no good after I'm a corpse.'

Slim and Les rode in, attracted by the shot, got some coffee, and rode away again. Hashknife picked up his bed-roll and led the way to a spot some distance away from where they had lain.

'There wasn't any ants over at our last place,' said Sleepy.

'I wasn't thinkin' about ants,' said Hashknife quietly. 'You'll notice that Shorty spread his roll just about where I was bedded when the ants drove us away.'

'Yuh mean—somebody was gunnin' for you?'

'Who would try to kill Shorty Hill?'

Sleepy was quiet for quite a while after he was inside his bed. Then he said, 'Do yuh reckon that telegram had anythin' to do with it?'

'That telegram merely asked us to get in touch with a certain man.'

'I know that,' replied Sleepy, 'but I never did trust Bob Marsh. Didn't yuh notice how Slim Sherrod acted? If yuh ask me—Slim knows Henry Webster.'

Hashknife chuckled. 'I wonder if knowing Henry is a sin.'

'Just like I said,' replied Sleepy, 'I don't trust Bob Marsh.'

CHAPTER II

AFTERNOON IN
ANTELOPE FLATS

IT WAS mid-afternoon in Antelope Flats, and the town dozed under a brassy sun. Saddle-horses were strung along the hitching-posts, and here and there were buggy teams and wagons. A few men sat in the shade of the Prong Horn Saloon. Joe Le Blanc, the blacksmith, his apron flung aside, sprawled in the shade of his shop and drank beer from a pail with Alphabet Anderson, who owned the livery-stable.

Jim Martin, the sheriff, walked heavily into his office, where Mañana Higgins, his deputy, sprawled on a cot reading a paper-back novel. Martin sat down at his desk and mopped his brow.

'I thought that damn dude and his valet was here,' he said.

'Oh, they went out quite a while ago,' sighed Mañana.

'I hope they stay out.'

Mañana marked his page with a strip of whang-leather and looked up. 'They won't,' he said quietly. 'The dude said he'd like to write the story of yore life.'

The sheriff stared at Mañana. 'The story of my life? Why, I—I ain't done anythin'.'

'Well,' said Mañana, 'mebbe I did pile it on a little thick.'

'Thick? Mañana, what did you tell him?'

'Oh, jist this and that. You know how it is.'

Jim Martin scratched his chin and studied Mañana. If there was anything Mañana loved to do it was to lie to some unsuspecting person.

'The story of my life, eh?' he said. 'How can he write the story of my life? I'm still alive.'

'Thasso?' queried Mañana. He marked the page of his novel and looked keenly at the sheriff. 'Uh-huh,' he said quietly. 'Mebbe yuh are.'

'Mebbe I am! Mañana, what in hell did you tell that dude about me?'

'Well,' replied Mañana thoughtfully, 'I started yuh out young. At the tender age of ten, you killed yore first man.'

'I never did!' snorted the sheriff. 'You lied to him. Who was the man?'

'Billy the Kid.'

'Mañana, yo're the biggest liar unhung. I never even seen Billy.'

'Yuh shot him in the dark. It was months afterward before yuh found out who yuh killed. You've probably forgot about it.'

'And you told him all that?'

'More,' nodded Mañana quietly. 'Before yuh was twenty-one you had killed twenty-one men.'

'You didn't expect him to believe that, did yuh, Mañana?'

'He said,' replied Mañana soberly, 'that he knowed the first time he ever seen yuh that you was a killer. He says yuh can always tell by their eyes.'

'Who told him that foolishness?'

'Artemus.'

'That little horse-thief. When's the dude goin' to write the book?'

'Yuh can't write a man's life until he's dead,' said Mañana soberly. 'Yuh can't tell what you might do before that, Jim. I sold him that old Colt of yours for seven dollars.'

'My old Colt? You've got a lot of gall, Mañana. Why, that gun is worth easy ten dollars—if it'd stay cocked.'

'It won't—but he don't know it.'

'Hell, he might kill himself with it!'

'That's why I took off two and a half on the price. I figure it would be dirt cheap.'

'Where'd they go from here?'

'He said they was goin' to the bank. He said, "Come, Artemus." Artemus! Smoky acts like he owned the earth. Some day I'm goin' to kick him in the seat of the pants so hard it'll straighten his legs.'

And because Antelope Flats was enjoying a siesta, no one saw three men ride in behind the bank and dismount quickly. Antelope Flats kept right on drowsing until they heard a fusillade of shots and some strident yelps. Jim Martin came to life, dived for his gun rack, and ran out into the street, levering a shell into the chamber.

Charles Stevens, the banker, was out on the sidewalk, brandishing a revolver and yelling, 'Holdup! Holdup!'

Right behind him came Alexander Hamilton Montgomery and Artemus. The three riders swept out from around the bank and into the street about two blocks from the entrance to the bank, running in a cloud of dust.

'There they go!' cried the banker, and shot a hole in the top of his porch. Alexander Hamilton Montgomery attempted to shoot, too, but the gun went off, and Joe Le Blanc, across the street, dived for cover when the bullet went through his beer pail.

Jim Martin steadied his heavy rifle against a porch post, notched his sights on that dust-cloud, and began throwing lead. He was guessing at the center of that cloud as he emptied his gun. Then he ran back into the office, grabbed his gun belt, and with Mañana right behind him they headed for the Prong Horn hitch-rack.

'We're borrowin' two horses!' he yelled at the men. No one denied him the right, as some of them ran for their horses, while others headed for the bank.

'They got twelve hundred dollars,' informed the excited banker.

Joe Le Blanc came running, still carrying the pail with the bullet hole through the middle. He panted: 'By gar, I'm theenk those sheriff hit one man! He is not able to sit up quite plain.'

'You think one of them got hit?' asked the banker.

'Sure. I see the other man grab him. I think he got hit.'

The crowd was soon augmented by several dozen more people, and Le Blanc elaborated his story up to a point where he saw one man completely shot out of his saddle, perhaps shot entirely in two, because he thought he saw each of the other men take a half. Le Blanc was not lacking in imagination.

The banker turned to Alexander Hamilton Montgomery and said, 'Well, you said you would like to witness a real Western bank robbery.'

'I—I feel very much as Aladdin must have felt the very first time he rubbed the lamp,' said the young man soberly. 'The—er—service was very good.'

It had been a long, hard ride up the Valley of the Lost Horse, and Hashknife and Sleepy were tired as they rode slowly, expecting at any time to find the town of Antelope Flats.

They came down from the rim of the hills,

where the road cut through a scattering of cotton-woods, and stopped to let their horses drink at a small stream.

'Nice range,' remarked Hashknife. 'Plenty feed.'

'You sure make it sound invitin',' sighed Sleepy. 'If we don't hit that town pretty soon, I'm goin' to try grass. I'm awful hungry.'

As they rode on, Hashknife looked at his old silver watch.

'We ought to reach Antelope Flats pretty soon,' he said.

'Yeah,' agreed Sleepy doubtfully. 'Twenty miles back was a sign that said it was twelve and a half miles to Antelope Flats. Why didn't they say twelve or thirteen miles, instead of usin' a fraction? They lied, anyway.'

The old road wound down through the dry-wash for about a mile and came out through a small clearing, where an old tumbledown fence partly enclosed an old shack. Lying in the middle of the road was the body of a man. Hashknife and Sleepy drew up quickly, searching the country for any sign of action. Neither of them spoke as they dismounted. The man was on his face, both arms outspread.

Hashknife studied the dust in the road, reading all the signs, before going to the body and turning it over. He was a young man, wearing cowboy garb. His gun had fallen from his holster and was in the dust.

'He was shot in the back,' said Hashknife. 'Never knew much about it, I don't suppose. The sign in the dirt says that he fell off his horse and rolled over. Horse might have been goin' fast, too.'

They went back to their horses, circled the body, and headed out across the valley. A mile or so farther brought them to the main road, where a sign said that Antelope Flats was only two miles away.

There seemed to be quite a lot of people on the street for this time of day, and they looked curiously at the two dust-covered riders who drew up in front of the sheriff's office. A man asked them if they were looking for the sheriff.

Hashknife replied, 'We found a dead man—and he looks as though he had been murdered.'

Several more men came down, and Hashknife explained where they had found the dead man.

'That's the old Byers place,' said one of them. 'Just this side of Hoodoo Wash. By golly, Le Blanc was right—the sheriff drilled one of them. We better get the coroner, and mebbe we'll pick up the sheriff. Him and Mañana went out of here hell-for-leather. He must have kept on the main road. Are yuh sure he's dead?'

'I'm afraid he is,' admitted Hashknife.

Jim Martin and Mañana Higgins pounded out of town on their borrowed horses, realizing the old proverb of the sea, 'A stern chase is a long chase,' but the sheriff had a feeling that at least one of his bullets had found a billet.

'If I missed all three of 'em—I was shootin' bad,' he told Mañana.

'Pretty hard to center anybody in that dust,' panted Mañana. 'If they hold to the road, we might find 'em—but they won't. I wonder how much money they got. Nervy devils! Didja see that dude in front of the bank, shootin' that old Colt? It's a wonder he didn't kill some innercent person.'

'You watch to the left and I'll watch to the right!' yelled the sheriff as they raced along.

They passed the road which led to the right, little used of late, and which led to the old Byers place. Mañana looked over that way, wondering if the pursued had gone in that direction. There was no reason for the robbers to keep to the road, knowing that there would be a chase; but what use of the two officers' leaving the road, not knowing just what the three men might do?

'We'll keep goin' awhile,' said the grim-faced sheriff. 'No use, of course, but we've got to do somethin'.'

For several miles they kept on going. Then they saw a dust-cloud ahead and put on more speed, only to find that it was a few head of cows crossing the dusty road. Finally the sheriff shook his head and drew up.

'It's no use, Mañana,' he said. 'They've cut off the road. Mebbe they cut into the brush right away.'

'It was a nice ride, anyway,' observed Mañana.

The sheriff led the way to the top of a mesa where they could look over the surrounding country, but there was nothing to be seen. It was evident to them that the three men had vanished.

'Do yuh still think yuh hit one of 'em, Jim?' asked Mañana.

'I don't know,' admitted the sheriff. 'That old Winchester shoots where yuh hold it at that distance; and I was sure in the middle of that dust.'

'Well, we might as well go back,' sighed Mañana. 'No use stayin' here.'

They did not hurry on the return journey. The sheriff was not too happy.

'They'll blame my office,' he said.

'Sure,' agreed Mañana. 'You should have been in the bank, settin' on a counter, with a cocked gun in yore hand. Negligence, I calls it.'

'That's right. Didja notice the colors of the horses they rode?'

'Nope,' replied Mañana. 'When folks start shootin'—I'm color-blind.'

'Same here. I hope they didn't get away with too much. That bank can't stand a big haul.'

'I've got seventeen dollars in there,' sighed Mañana. 'I ort to know better.'

Slowly they rode back toward Antelope Flats,

and as they approached the road which led to the Byers place, they saw several men on horseback and a wagon coming onto the main road. They spurred quickly ahead and drew up beside the cavalcade.

The men were all from Antelope Flats; men who were there when the robbery occurred.

One of them said, 'A coupla strangers came in over this road, Sheriff, and they found him.'

'Found who?' asked the sheriff gruffly.

'The man you shot,' replied the man quietly. 'We've got him in the wagon. It's Dean Harder. He must have died in his saddle.'

'My Gawd!' whispered Mañana—but the sheriff did not say anything.

CHAPTER III

'DO YOU KNOW A MAN NAMED HENRY WEBSTER?'

NO ONE asked Hashknife and Sleepy to go along, so they stabled their tired horses and secured a room at the old hotel before seeking food. The elderly proprietor, Andy Vincent, told them about the bank robbery, and that the blacksmith noted that one of the men was injured.

'You must have been just short of meetin' 'm,' he said. 'They might have took a shot at yuh.'

'They might,' smiled Hashknife. 'Do you know a man named Henry Webster?'

'No, I don't reckon I ever did.'

'Lived here long?'

'I've been runnin' this hotel for thirty years.'

'And you never knew Henry Webster. We heard he lived here.'

'Son,' said Vincent patronizingly, 'when you live to my age you'll learn to misbelieve everythin' yuh hear. And when yuh get my age yore eyes will be so bad that yuh won't believe half yuh think you see. This world is plumb full of misleadin' information. There ain't been no Henry Webster around here for thirty years that I know of.'

They went outside and sat down on the shady porch.

'Can it be that Bob Marsh is also a liar?' asked Sleepy.

'My gosh!' exclaimed Hashknife. 'Here comes Monty and his valet!'

'And Monty,' added Sleepy, 'is packin' a gun.'

They came down the sidewalk with Artemus about three steps to the rear, and stopped near Hashknife and Sleepy.

'My goodness!' exclaimed Alexander Hamilton Montgomery. Artemus grinned and adjusted his misfit hat.

'How do yuh like Antelope Flats?' asked Hashknife.

'Exciting place,' replied Montgomery. 'Very, very exciting.'

'Bank robberies and everythin',' added Artemus.

'We were in the bank,' said Montgomery.

'And,' added Artemus, 'Mr. Montgomery shot at the bandits and damn near killed the blacksmith.'

A team and buckboard drew up at the front of the general store next door, driven by a very pretty and capable-looking young lady.

Artemus whispered, 'That's Sally Harder, daughter of the meanest old devil that ever made a track in the sand.'

Sally tied one of the horses to a porch post,

glanced at the four men, and went into the store.

'Old Flint Harder owns the Quarter-Circle H spread,' said Artemus. 'He's a cripple, and he hates the world. Him and Jim Martin, the sheriff, hated each other for years. Years ago Jim Martin mistook Harder for an outlaw and busted him with a coupla bullets. Not long ago Dean, Flint Harder's son, married the sheriff's daughter.'

'Complicated things, eh?' queried Hashknife.

'They tell me,' nodded Artemus, and had to adjust his hat again.

Sally Harder came out and drove away.

Artemus said: 'She's prob'ly been out to Dean's little ranch. They tell me Flint is dead-set against her bein' friendly with them, but Sally laughs at him and keeps on goin' out there.'

'I should like to meet her,' said Montgomery quietly.

'Wait'll yuh meet her pa,' suggested Artemus.

'I,' said Montgomery, 'am not interested in her father.'

'Yuh might be. Old Flint was so damn mad about Dean gettin' married that he said he'd shoot the first damn fool that came monkeyin' around Sally.'

'I am no damn fool,' said Montgomery stiffly.

Artemus shrugged again, and had to lift his hat off his eyes.

'Why don't yuh stuff some newspaper into the band of that hat?' asked Sleepy.

39

Before Artemus could reply, Andy Vincent spoke from the doorway.

'I reckon they're bringin' the body in.'

A number of riders were escorting a wagon, which turned down a side street. Two of the riders came on and stopped in front of the hotel.

One of the men said, 'The dead man was Dean Harder, Andy.'

'Dean Harder!' exclaimed the hotel man. 'No!'

'Yeah. Shot through the back. I reckon the others held him in the saddle as long as they could.'

'The sheriff's son-in-law,' said Andy Vincent. 'That's awful.'

'And Flint Harder's son,' added the other man.

'What did Jim Martin say?' asked Vincent.

'Not a word. He turned the color of alkali dust, but he didn't say a thing. But nobody can blame him. He was throwin' lead at bank robbers.'

'No, they can't blame him,' agreed Vincent. 'He didn't know who they were.'

Vincent sat down in a chair and mopped his brow.

'Dean always was as wild as a hawk,' he said, 'but I didn't think he'd do that. Nell Martin is a fine girl. Jim didn't want her to marry Dean, and Flint didn't want Dean to marry Nell. They eloped. Flint gave Dean a little ranch and a few head of cows, and told him to go to hell. Mebbe

40

Dean needed money. I heard he was havin' a hard time gettin' along.'

A young cowboy came from the Prong Horn Saloon, crossed the street, and headed in the direction taken by the wagon.

'That's Danny Long,' said Vincent. 'He owns a little ranch near Dean's place. Him and his wife are awful good friends of Dean and Nell. Danny is one feller that ain't scared to talk with Flint Harder. Danny hates the whole Quarter-Circle H outfit. There goes Swede Olson, followin' Danny. He works for Danny, and he's always just about that far behind him. Funny old Swede. Packs a cap-and-ball Colt that won't stay cocked. He'll kill himself some day.'

They were silent for a while, and finally Alexander Hamilton Montgomery said, 'Speaking of guns which will not stay cocked—do they always kill their owner?'

'Not always,' replied Hashknife soberly. 'That's the trouble with them.'

Artemus chuckled and his hat slid down again.

Sleepy said, 'You shouldn't buy a seven and a quarter hat for a six and seven-eighths head.'

'I like 'em comfortable,' said Artemus.

'Here comes the sheriff and deputy,' said Vincent.

Jim Martin was a big man, with heavy features, long, dangling arms, and big feet. He walked as a man walks in loose sand, looking straight ahead.

He never looked at or spoke to the men in front of the hotel. Mañana Higgins was tall and lean, with the stiff-legged walk of a man who had spent most of his life in the saddle. He looked at the men, but said nothing.

Hashknife sighed and tossed his cigarette into the street.

'Life's a queer thing,' he said quietly. 'You can't dodge Fate. That sheriff couldn't help doin' what he did. Dean Harder couldn't help what he did. Circumstances lead up to such things. Dean Harder was disowned for marryin' Martin's daughter. He needed money, because his father wouldn't help him over the rough road. So he took the wrong way out of it. Fate put Jim Martin into the thing; put a gun in his hand in time to down the one man he didn't want to down. I believe it was all written in the book.'

'What book?' asked Vincent.

'A book that we will never see,' replied Hashknife. 'Our names are in it, and opposite each name is a date and a cause. You can't dodge it. There was a feller named Omar, long ago, who wrote somethin' about it. I don't remember the exact words, but it said, "The movin' finger writes, and havin' writ, moves on; nor all yore piety nor wit can cancel half a line, nor all yore tears wash out one word of it." I ain't sure about the wordin', but that's close enough for me.'

'You've got queer ideas, Hartley,' said Vincent.

42

'I've seen queer things,' replied Hashknife.

'A feller could keep from robbin' a bank if he wanted to.'

'If he did—his book showed a different entry.'

'I think you've got a screw loose,' said Vincent. 'You try that on a Lost Horse jury and see what they do. We deal in cold, hard facts down in this country.'

Vincent went back into the hotel. Alexander Hamilton Montgomery and Artemus had been interested listeners.

Montgomery said: 'That is an interesting theory, Mr. Hartley. I wonder if the book you mention has an entry after my name saying that I am destined to write a great play.'

'That book,' replied Hashknife, 'likely contains a lot of remarkable entries.'

'If I was you,' said Artemus, 'I'd git the hammer fixed on that gun. Yuh could do that much for yourself, in spite of what's in the book.'

'That is correct,' admitted Montgomery. 'I shall get that trigger fixed at once—or is it the hammer? Anyway, it was fun for a moment. I ran out of the bank with Mr. Stevens just as the three men were riding away, with everyone yelling. Then I remembered that I had a gun; so I drew it out, pulled back the hammer—and it went off.'

'And almost killed the blacksmith,' reminded Artemus dryly. 'If I was you I'd take it back to the sheriff's office and get my money back.'

'I bought it in good faith,' said Montgomery. 'He allowed me to examine it. No, it was my own fault. Mr. Hartley, I rather like your theory about our future being written in a book. It seems better that way, instead of being—er—creatures going willy-nilly, with no definite goal, as you might say. Every time I have something happen to me now, I shall say, "It was there in the book; so there was no use in my trying to do it differently." Whatever I do, I know that is what I should have done.'

'And forgive those who trespass against you?' queried Hashknife soberly.

'Trespass against me? Why—by Jove, if they do, they are merely going according to what is written about them. The theory has enormous possibilities—for and against.'

'It has,' agreed Hashknife.

'Where did you learn it?' asked Montgomery.

Hashknife smiled slowly. 'Along the ridges, down in the canyons, in the cow-camps, beside the water-holes—any old place.'

'Not in a school?'

'They don't teach that theory in a school,' said Hashknife.

'I still think,' said Artemus, 'that you'd better get that hammer fixed. It might save a life.'

'I just happened to think,' said Montgomery quickly. 'That pretty girl is the sister of the slain bank robber!'

'That's right,' agreed Sleepy.

'That is terrible. I—I wish I might have a chance to tell her how sorry I am.'

'Yes,' agreed Artemus, 'you might ride out to the Quarter-Circle H and tell her. And after we get through pickin' the shot out of yore anatomy, you'll still be awful sorry.'

'Artemus,' said Montgomery, 'are you presuming to tell *me* what to do?'

'Well,' replied Artemus stoutly, 'as long as I'm supposed to learn yuh things about the West, I kinda feel responsible. I've been shot twice, tromped on by a bronc, and kicked into a hospital by a mule—and married a woman through pity. Outside of bein' kicked out of a couple colleges, you ain't been scratched yet. I feel just as sorry as you do, but I'm not goin' plumb out to the Quarter-Circle H filled with sympathy and come back filled with shot. I *know* Flint Harder.'

'What do you think, Mr. Hartley?' asked Montgomery.

'I believe I'd take the advice of Artemus.'

'Thank you. Come, Artemus.'

They went into the hotel. The two men who had talked with Vincent came across the street.

One of them said to Hashknife, 'When you found Dean Harder's body, yuh didn't see a horse around there, did yuh?'

'There wasn't any horse in sight,' replied Hashknife.

45

'Uh-huh. We saw yore tracks, where yuh turned him over. They just let him fall when they knew he was dead, I reckon. I'd hate to be in reach of old Flint Harder when he finds it out. He hated Jim Martin plenty before this happened; so he won't hate him any less.'

'Old Flint don't have to work hard to hate folks,' said the other.

Hashknife said, 'Do you gentlemen know a man named Henry Webster?'

They both shook their heads.

One said: 'I never heard of him. What does he do?'

'I don't know,' replied Hashknife. 'Did Les Hart work around here?'

'Yeah, he worked for Flint Harder quite a while. I dunno where he went.'

'Slim Sherrod worked here too, didn't he?'

'Yeah, he worked for Harder too. Slim left here about two months ago. Les left here before that. Do you know 'em?'

'Yeah, we worked with them on the UF spread, down in the Isabella country.'

The two men went into the hotel. Hashknife and Sleepy went down to a little restaurant, where everybody was discussing the killing of Dean Harder and what Flint Harder would do about it. About an hour later they were sitting in front of the hotel again, enjoying the cool breeze of early evening, when a buckboard team turned

46

down the side street. There were three people on the seat, and one was a woman.

'That's the same rig Sally Harder was drivin',' said Sleepy.

In a few minutes the equipage came back, with only the two men on the seat. It required little deduction to determine that one of them was Flint Harder. He was of medium size, gaunt and grizzled, and with a face so deeply lined that it might have been carved from granite. He cursed his driver, who happened to be Nick Higby, his foreman, for not getting out fast enough, but the big cowboy paid no attention to the profanity.

Harder scowled at Hashknife and Sleepy as he twisted painfully and got out of the seat, using a heavy cane. Higby started to assist him, but he shoved him aside, swore painfully, and managed to reach a seat on the porch. In spite of his crippled condition, he wore high-heel boots and carried a holstered gun.

Higby spoke quietly to him, and Harder said: 'I don't care what yuh do. Go to hell, as far as I'm concerned.'

Nick Higby walked away.

Harder shifted his eyes and looked at Hashknife and Sleepy. He growled: 'Tall and short one, eh? So you found him, eh?'

'If it's any of yore business—yes,' replied Hashknife calmly.

'Any of my business? Why, damn yore hides, I—I'm Flint Harder!'

'Is that name supposed to scare the children?' asked Sleepy.

'Scare the—' Flint Harder stared at Sleepy. 'What are you talkin' about?'

Hashknife looked at Harder and smiled slowly.

It infuriated Harder. 'Somethin' damn funny, eh? Man with a busted hip—that's funny.'

'Yore son was killed today—and you brag about yore own ailments,' said Hashknife quietly. 'You should be ashamed.'

Flint Harder flinched visibly, turned away and looked across the street. For once in his life he had no retort on the end of his tongue. Jim Martin, the sheriff, was coming up the street. Flint Harder saw him, and his right hand slid to the butt of his holstered gun. The sheriff did not look up. Flint Harder slid his gun loose and clicked back the hammer, but Hashknife's left hand clamped viselike on his wrist, while his right hand tore the gun away. The sheriff stopped and looked at Harder, who was clawing at Hashknife's sleeve, trying to get the gun.

'You damn meddlin' fool!' he rasped.

'No shootin', if yuh please,' said Hashknife.

'I came here to kill you, Martin,' said Harder, 'but this meddlin' fool took my gun.'

Jim Martin looked at Hashknife and said quietly, 'Give him back his gun—it's all right.'

'Two fools don't justify murder,' said Hash-knife.

'He killed my son,' gritted Harder.

'He killed a bank robber,' corrected Hashknife.

'He was my daughter's husband,' said the sheriff.

'Another killin' won't bring him back—nor help his widow,' said Hashknife. 'You've both lost—why not bury the hatchet?'

'I'd bury it—in his damned head!' snarled Harder. 'Give me back that gun. This ain't none of yore damn business. He's got a gun.'

Hashknife smiled and looked at the sheriff.

'Do you two want to shoot it out?' he asked.

The sheriff looked at Harder and his eyes narrowed. 'Shoot it out with that damn cripple? No! When I shoot it out with a man, I want him physically and mentally right.'

The sheriff went on up the street, leaving Flint Harder to squirm in his chair and glare at Hashknife. When the sheriff was a distance away, Hashknife removed the cartridges from the gun and handed it back to Harder, who shoved it into his holster.

'Just who in hell are you?' he asked.

'I'm the man who kept you from makin' a fool of yourself.'

'Pretty smart, eh? Keep yore nose out of my business or you'll get it shot off.'

'Tough people,' said Sleepy.

Alexander Hamilton Montgomery and Artemus came out of the hotel, and Montgomery came straight to Flint Harder.

'Mr. Vincent told me that you are Mr. Harder,' he said. 'I am Alexander Hamilton Montgomery, and I wanted to tell you how sorry I am. You see, I was in the bank at the time. To your charming daughter I should like to have you convey my deepest—'

'Shut up!' roared Flint Harder. 'You—you—' Flint Harder's voice sank to a reedy whisper. 'Get away from me you—you—'

'I beg your pardon, sir,' said Montgomery. 'I didn't realize—come, Artemus.'

'I told yuh,' said Artemus. 'In time, you'll learn.'

They went down the street. Flint Harder drew a deep breath.

'I heard about them two,' he said. 'Artemus! That damn Smoky Day puttin' on airs. Stole horses for twenty years—and look at him now!'

'Mr. Harder,' said Hashknife, 'you've lived here a long time, haven't yuh?'

'Too damn long!' snapped Harder.

'Did you ever know a man named Henry Webster?'

'Huh? Henry Webster? What about him?'

'Did you ever know him?' asked Sleepy.

'Maybe you can tell me where I can find him,' suggested Hashknife.

Flint Harder scowled thoughtfully over the question. Finally he said: 'The last time I seen him, I told him to go to hell. If he ain't there, I don't know where you'll find him.'

'What business was he in?' asked Hashknife.

'He tried to get into mine. Well, here comes Nick Higby. I'm glad I don't have to set here and listen to you fellers yap any longer. That's the worst of bein' a cripple—yuh can't walk away.'

He got to his feet and hobbled out to the buckboard. Sleepy tried to assist him, but he snarled like a wolf: 'When I want help. I'll ask for it. Get to hell out of here, before I shoot somebody.'

'That's a bad habit,' remarked Hashknife.

Flint Harder twisted in his seat and scowled at Hashknife. 'Shootin' people?' he asked.

'No—talkin' about it,' replied Hashknife. 'You know what they say about barkin' dogs.'

Nick Higby seemed on the point of laughter as he backed the team and turned around. Few ever talked back to Flint Harder.

'Wormwood and gall,' sighed Sleepy as they drove away.

Hashknife smiled. 'At least, we know that there was a man named Henry Webster, Sleepy.'

'And we know where he was told to go,' said Sleepy soberly. 'Yuh might write to Bob March and give him the address.'

After supper that evening, Alexander Hamilton

51

Montgomery came to Hashknife in the little hotel lobby.

'I have given Artemus the evening off—for drinking purposes,' said the young man.

'For drinkin' purposes?' queried Hashknife, a bit puzzled.

'Yes. You see, Artemus has his periods. I made him promise not to drink while on duty; so at intervals I allow him an evening off for his own indulgence.'

'Uh-huh, I see. Quite an idea.'

'My own,' nodded Montgomery proudly.

'This is your first trip West?' asked Hashknife.

'I went to college in Berkeley, until they kicked me out. It was my second experience of that kind, and Dad said it was the last. When I suggested coming West for material for a play, Dad was enthusiastic. He is very fond of the theater, you see. He said that if I could write a successful play, he would—well, he mentioned a million dollars.'

'Yore father has plenty of money, I reckon.'

'Why, yes, I suppose he has. I really can't say how much.'

'Why don't yuh ask him for enough to buy a big ranch and start raisin' cows?'

'I never thought of that. By Jove, it would be an experience!'

'On second thought,' said Hashknife, 'you should wait until you have written that play, and then use yore reward money.'

Montgomery nodded slowly. 'It might be better. By the way, Mr. Harder was, I felt, very rude today.'

'Yeah, he wasn't very nice,' agreed Hashknife.

'Peculiar nationality,' said Montgomery.

'Yeah?' queried Hashknife.

'Yes. Artemus says he is a cross between a vinegaroon and a sidewinder.'

'That's quite a mixture,' said Hashknife soberly.

'Indeed, yes. By the way, to what tribe do you belong, Mr. Hartley?'

'Tribe?' asked Hashknife curiously.

'Well, perhaps I should not have mentioned it, but Artemus said you looked like a good Indian. Injun, I believe he called it.'

'Thank Artemus for me,' smiled Hashknife.

'Tomorrow Artemus is going to get us each a horse and saddle. He says I must learn to ride. Perhaps we will go out to the Harder home. I should like to have a talk with Miss Harder, even if her father was rude to me. She needs a friend, they say.'

'Who says?' queried Hashknife.

'Why, I heard it in the store. They said her only friend was a Mrs. Long.'

'Pardner,' said Hashknife, 'you take my advice and stay away from that ranch. If she wants you, I'm sure she'll send for yuh.'

'But she doesn't even know me, Mr. Hartley.'

'That's just it—she might make a mistake.'

53

'I see,' murmured Montgomery. 'Well, of course, I do not want to go where I am not wanted—but I'm not sure about that. But it doesn't seem right for a girl like that to have only one friend. She is too charming not to have friends.'

'Don't believe everything you hear,' warned Hashknife. 'Some of these folks draw a long bow.'

'Draw a long bow? Oh, I see—an Indian symbol.'

'Yeah,' agreed Hashknife, 'I suppose.'

'Do you know,' remarked Montgomery, 'I am beginning to like folks out here. They are very frank. I must admit that few of them are well dressed or well bartered, but it doesn't seem to matter.'

'It ain't how yuh look—it's how yuh act,' said Hashknife.

'I realize that more every day. They call me a dude, and I am trying to dress and act like them. How long does one have to live here in order to be accepted?'

'You'll have to count yore own time, Monty. You think they're laughin' at you—and they think you're laughin' at them.'

'Really? But I'm not. I admire those slim-waisted cowboys who need a shave and a haircut. I like the way they walk along on those damnable high heels, with their spurs jingling. Their chaps fit—mine don't. Why, I can't even make a gun hang as they do. And the way they get onto a horse! Even Artemus makes me ashamed. I'm not ignorant—I hope—but I doubt that I'll ever learn the rudiments of riding.'

'They'd be lost in a city,' said Hashknife. 'Monty, those boys never done anythin' in their lives except ride a horse and work cattle. It's all they know. Very few of them have any book education. They're frank, because they are not civilized enough to lie to yuh. They don't dislike yuh. They're just wonderin' why yo're too dumb to know how to handle a horse.'

'You are also frank,' smiled Montgomery.

'Why not?' queried the tall cowboy. 'I'm one of 'em, Monty.'

'I realize that, Mr. Hartley. The first time I ever saw you mount a horse, I became jealous. And the way you carry a gun, with the handle of it sticking out an angle, and looking as though it was ready to fall. Why do you wear it that way?'

Hashknife smiled slowly. 'When I want a gun,' he said quietly, 'I don't want to have to go too far to get it, Monty.'

'I see. Well, I shall learn all these things in time, I suppose.'

'You will,' agreed Hashknife, 'because you use your eyes.'

CHAPTER IV

SWEDE OLSON NEEDS SOME GIN

DANNY LONG rode back from the Dean Harder ranch, where his wife was staying with Nell Harder. Danny and Dean had been friends all their lives, and even after their marriages they were almost inseparable. The death of Dean was a terrible shock to Danny and his wife, and he was a grim-faced young cowboy as he rode back to his own ranch that morning.

The fact that Nell's father had killed her husband was one of the bad points to the incident. Danny liked the sheriff, and he wanted to make things as easy for him as possible, but when he tried to explain to Nell that her father was not to blame, Danny's wife had berated him for suggesting that Dean, being the thief, was entirely to blame.

Danny rode home, wondering what he *should* have said. Swede Olson was just leaving the ranch to repair a piece of drift-fence, and saw Danny arrive. Swede waved and rode on. That break in the drift-fence had been there for months. Normally it would have been ignored for more months, but Swede wanted to do something; to get away from arguing over what had happened.

Danny sat on the porch for a few minutes, but suddenly decided to go to town and see what had developed. There would be an inquest, and he wanted to be there. Danny started down to the stable, when a crow alighted on the ridge of the stable and cawed at him, defiantly, it seemed.

'Maybe yo're the bad luck around here,' said Danny. He drew his gun and took a snap shot at the crow, which went away cawing wildly, most of its tail feathers missing. Danny chuckled and went on to get his horse.

Swede Olson heard that shot. He was not too far away to realize that it had been fired at the ranch-house. There was nothing unusual about the sound of a shot in a country where all men carried guns, but Swede turned his horse around and started in the direction of the ranch-house.

'Ay guess Ay am yust getting yumpy,' he told his horse.

Danny was not at the house, nor was his horse. Swede fanned himself with his hat, decided it was too hot to work anyway, and took his horse down to the stable. He unsaddled, tied his horse in a stall, and started to climb up to the hayloft to toss down some hay, when he happened to notice a surplus of hay already in the manger. The horse snorted a little and pulled back the length of its tie-rope.

Swede came down, shoved past the horse, and looked into the manger. Then he shoved some of the hay aside, jerked back quickly, and walked to the doorway, where he took off his hat and fanned himself again. Swede's ruddy face was beaded with perspiration.

'Ay vill be damned!' he exclaimed aloud. 'Ay yust vill be!'

With fumbling fingers he fished out a small box of snuff from his shirt-pocket, and with a sufficient quantity stuffed inside his upper lip, he sat down on the sill and pondered the situation. There was a man stuffed into that manger and covered with hay. He had heard the shot that killed the man. Danny had been the only one at the ranch when the shot was fired. Now, Danny was gone and there was a dead man in the manger. After ten minutes of reflection, Swede said:

'Ay vill be damned!'

Evidently he had arrived at a decision. He saddled his horse and put a blindfold over its eyes. Swede Olson was a powerful man. He lifted the body from the manger and placed it across his saddle, while with a lariat he quickly bound it there. Then he led the horse outside and removed the covering from its eyes. Satisfied that the coast was clear, he led the horse through a side gate and down through the brush, following an old cow-trail.

Artemus Day was having his troubles. He had purchased two horses and saddles for himself and Alexander Hamilton Montgomery, and now he was trying to teach Montgomery the art of mounting a horse. Twice after getting his foot in the stirrup the horse had whirled and left the young tenderfoot flat on his back in the sand.

Disheveled and panting, Montgomery demanded to know the secret.

'Yuh see,' explained Artemus, 'in gettin' on a horse, yuh have to get on the left side—not the right.'

Montgomery shook his head, trying to shake some sand from his collar. 'And you let me keep on trying to get on the wrong side,' he said reprovingly.

'Well, I'll tell yuh,' drawled Artemus, 'I've allus felt that the way to learn a feller anythin' is to let him do it wrong a few times.'

'If he doesn't break his neck,' added Montgomery.

'In that case—school is out,' said Artemus. 'Try it again.'

The next attempt was a success, and they rode slowly out of Antelope Flats, heading in the general direction of Danny Long's ranch.

'Don't be so tight,' advised Artemus. 'You won't fall off. Let yourself swing with the horse. Don't hold a rein in each hand; leave 'em both in yore left hand. If yuh want to turn either way, just swing yore hand out or in, and let the rein fall against his neck.'

'Simple, isn't it?' smiled Montgomery. 'I love it, Artemus. I feel so high up in the air.'

'You'll prob'ly go higher'n that before yuh ride very long.'

They didn't ride faster than a slow trot, although Montgomery suggested a faster pace.

'I got yuh up there, and I want yuh to stay awhile,' declared Artemus. 'You'll have plenty time to ride fast after yuh find out how to stay on.'

'There is really nothing to it, once you are on the saddle,' said Montgomery.

'Yeah, that's right. Just be sure yuh stay there, until yuh *want* to get off.'

Artemus led the way off the road and they traveled cattle-trails. The little bowlegged ex-cowboy pointed out cattle and explained about the brands. He showed Montgomery a coyote slinking along the side of a hill, hardly more than a shadow in the desert growth; and a desert rattler taking a siesta in the shade of a bush.

'It is marvelous,' sighed Montgomery; 'but this saddle becomes rather hard after a while.'

'You'll eat like a horse for a few days,' said Artemus soberly.

'Like a horse? How is that, Artemus?'

'Standin' up,' replied the little cowboy dryly.

They rode around the point of a hill and down through a trail which led through a forest of mesquite.

They broke into an opening and almost ran into a man leading a horse. The man stepped back past the horse and ran as fast as he could through the mesquite. For some distance they could hear him running, but the sound died away in the distance. A few mesquite bushes blocked them from a good view of the horse.

'I'll be a dry-nurse to a dinny-sour!' exclaimed Artemus. 'What went wrong with that *hombre*?'

'He ran away and left his horse,' said Montgomery. 'Very strange.'

'I hope to tell yuh. I've heard of a man's horse runnin' away from him, but I never heard it vicy-versa. Huh!'

Artemus spurred ahead and they rode around to the horse. What they saw caused them to pull up quickly. There was the body of a man roped to the saddle. Artemus dismounted and gingerly approached the animal, hunched down as he tried to see the face of the dead man.

'Lon Porter!' he exclaimed. 'It's Lon Porter.'

'Is he—is he—dead?' faltered Montgomery.

'Deader'n a doorknob,' replied Artemus.

'Who is Lon Porter?'

'He—he was a puncher at the Quarter-Circle H. Hell, I knowed him a long time. Well, well! Lon Porter.'

'It—it rather makes me sick,' said Montgomery. 'I don't believe I ever saw a dead man before. What do you suppose caused him to die, Artemus?'

'I dunno. It kinda looks like somebody killed him, and was takin' him out to a private burin' ground.'

'You mean—he was murdered?'

'I ain't no Seventh Son,' replied Artemus, 'but even down here we don't approve of folks doin' a killin' and their own private buryin'.'

Montgomery sat down in the shade of a bush and soberly contemplated the dead man on the horse, while Artemus rolled a cigarette, his hat on the back of his head.

'You say that this man was a cowboy with the Harder outfit?' asked Montgomery.

'Uh-huh,' nodded Artemus, blowing a streamer of smoke from his nostrils. 'He'd been with the Harder outfit quite a while. Nice fellow.'

'He had enemies, I suppose, Artemus.'

'This country is funny, of course,' said Artemus, 'but I ain't never heard of a man killin' his friend. I been a-settin' here, tryin' to figure out a first-class enemy for Lon Porter. Yuh got to hate a man quite a lot before yuh kill him. At least, that's my code.'

'You have killed a man?' queried Montgomery.

'I never convict myself,' replied Artemus, 'but I will say that many a man has felt my bullets. I ain't what you'd call a regular killer. I'm hard to rouse—but I'm bad when yuh git me mad. I never ask nor give quarter.'

'I didn't know you had a bad disposition, Artemus.'

'Don't rub me the wrong way,' advised the little cowboy.

'Oh, I never intend to do that,' said Montgomery quickly. 'Do you know who owns that horse?'

'Oh—the horse. Lemme see.'

Artemus walked around the animal and examined the brands. It was marked in three different places, but Artemus didn't recognize any of the brand-marks. He shook his head and came back to Montgomery.

'I jist figure that somebody mowed him down, tied him on a horse, and was goin' to bury him out in the hills. He's deader'n a doorknob, and we can't help him none. Personally, I don't like to monkey with another man's funeral plans.'

'But—but what are we going to do with him, Artemus? After all, it is none of our affair.'

'If we had any sense,' said Artemus, 'we'd ride away and forget it—but we ain't.'

'Ain't we?' asked Montgomery.

Artemus looked curiously at Montgomery. 'Yo're learnin',' he said approvingly.

'What do you mean, Artemus?'

'Learnin' to talk right. You just said "ain't." '

Artemus rode over, picked up the long lead-rope, and took a loop around his saddle-horn.

'We're takin' him to town,' he said. 'I'll take

the lead, and you foller. If he falls off, you can pick him up.'

'If I do not fall off first,' said Montgomery soberly.

Danny Long reached Antelope Flats just in time to attend the inquest. He heard Hashknife and Sleepy testify to finding the body, and also heard the sheriff, in a halting voice, tell of firing the shots at the departing outlaws. The banker was unable to identify any of them, nor did anyone seem to remember the colors of the horses they rode. Joe Le Blanc testified that he saw one of the riders sway in his saddle, and saw one of the other riders prevent him from falling.

Neither Flint Harder nor Sally came to the inquest, but Nick Higby and two of their cowboys were in attendance. Jim Martin, the sheriff, was exonerated of any blame in the matter. After the inquest Hashknife was talking with Mañana Higgins, the deputy, when Nick Higby came to them and asked if Mañana had seen Lon Porter.

'I ain't seen him for a coupla days, Nick,' replied Mañana.

'That's shore funny,' remarked Nick.

'You don't mean to say yo're so careless that you've lost a cowboy, do yuh?' asked Mañana.

'Lost, strayed, or stolen,' laughed Nick. 'He started for town last evenin', and we ain't seen him since.'

65

'Lon is a man-sized drinker,' said Mañana, 'and that might keep him among the missin' for a while; but he'll come home when he gets hungry.'

'Yeah, I reckon so,' agreed Nick. He turned to Hashknife and said: 'I reckon you told Flint Harder a few things yesterday. All the way back to the ranch he was thinkin' up new cuss words to call yuh. He said you stopped him from shootin' Jim Martin.'

'Would he have killed Martin?' asked Hashknife.

'I don't know. You never can tell about a man like Harder.'

Hashknife and Sleepy sat down in the shade with Mañana Higgins.

'Queer man, that Flint Harder,' said Mañana. 'He thinks the whole world is against him.'

'A deputy shot him by mistake, they tell me,' remarked Hashknife.

'That's right.'

'Did it happen here in Lost Horse Valley?'

'It shore did—and Jim Martin was the deputy.'

'No wonder he hates Jim Martin.'

'Well, it was a mistake, but Harder never believed it—not openly. He's always howlin' about somebody stealin' his cows. Told me he was goin' to ask the Association to send in a detective, but if he did, I never seen the detective.'

'Do you think he is really losin' cows, or does he just want to yelp about somethin'?'

'I don't know,' replied Mañana soberly. 'I didn't think so, until Bob Reynolds, owner of the Rockin' R, said he was losin' cows, too. I'd believe him quicker than I would Flint Harder.'

Danny Long came along, and Mañana introduced him to Hashknife and Sleepy. Mañana questioned him about Mrs. Dean Harder.

Danny said: 'It's awful tough on her, Mañana. It's bad enough to have her dead husband branded a thief, but it's worse to know her own father done the shootin'.'

'Was Dean short of money?' asked Mañana.

'Yeah, he was. We're all hard up, as far as that goes, but I didn't think Dean would go in for that kinda stuff. He didn't run around with a bad gang.'

'Wouldn't his father help him out?' asked Hashknife.

'That old sidewinder? Have you met him?'

'Yesterday,' smiled Hashknife. 'We had quite a talk.'

'He was goin' to shoot Jim Martin, but Hartley took his gun away,' said Mañana.

'That's the answer,' sighed Danny. 'Flint hates the world—and that includes Dean's wife. I don't know how anybody can hate Nell—but he does a pretty good job of it. Well, I've got to be driftin'. Glad to—'

'My Gawd, what have we here?' blurted Mañana.

It was Alexander Hamilton Montgomery and Artemus, with the body of Lon Porter. Alexander tried to dismount, caught his right spur in his saddle-skirt, and sat down ungracefully and heavily behind his horse.

Artemus looked at him in amazement as he said, 'You can find more ways of gettin' off than anybody I ever knew.'

Men crowded around them, questioning, arguing. Nick Higby and the sheriff shoved their way to the pack-horse. Hashknife and Sleepy stood on the wooden sidewalk, which gave them a view over the heads of the crowd.

Artemus Day was right in his element—the spotlight. He told his story, with gestures. Then the sheriff and Nick Higby took the lead-rope and headed for the doctor's house, while the crowd filed in behind, all except Alexander Hamilton Montgomery, who limped over to the sidewalk. Alphabetical Anderson had taken Montgomery's horse to the stable.

'Pardner,' said Hashknife to Montgomery, 'you seem to have had yore ups and downs today.'

'I got on and off several times,' replied the young man painfully. 'You saw my last dismount? That was quite an improvement over the others.'

'One thing,' remarked Sleepy dryly, 'when you get off, you get off all in a bunch. Nothin' lingerin'-like in it at all.'

'I leave nothing to the imagination,' nodded Montgomery. 'What an experience! Bringing in a dead man!'

'Artemus seemed to enjoy it,' remarked Sleepy.

'I hate to say it,' said the young man, 'but at times Artemus seems to display a crude sense of humor.'

'Was that yore first experience with a horse and saddle?' asked Sleepy.

'Yes. I am afraid to sit down, because I know I shall never get up again, and I am afraid to walk, because I really haven't any control of my limbs. I asked Artemus about it, and he said that is why so many men die out here with their boots on—they cannot get them off.'

'I've often wondered about that,' said Hash-knife.

They saw Danny Long ride out of town, and in a few minutes Jim Martin, the sheriff, and Mañana Higgins came down there.

'Who owned that Circle JR horse?' asked Hashknife.

'Danny Long,' replied Mañana. 'It's Swede Olson's saddle-horse. We've got to find Swede.'

'Would there be any reason for Swede killin' Lon Porter?'

Mañana shrugged his shoulders. 'Lon was shot in the back,' he said.

'Did Swede ever have any trouble with the Quarter-Circle H outfit?'

'Not personally. Danny and Flint Harder have had words, but everybody has had words with Flint Harder—even you, Hartley.'

'That's right.'

Mañana joined the sheriff in the office, and in a few minutes they got their horses and headed for the Long ranch. Hashknife and Sleepy helped Montgomery up to the hotel, and were sitting in the shade of the porch when Swede Olson came to town, riding a flea-bitten mule, sans saddle or bridle, with only a rope looped around its nose.

The sheriff's office was closed, so he booted the mule up in front of the hotel.

'Ay vant to see de sheriff,' he said nervously. 'Ay have been robbed.'

'Robbed of what?' asked Hashknife.

'My hurse and saddle. Ay vars fixing fence, and Ay saw a man take my hurse; so Ay had to ride de mule.'

'Tie yore mule and set awhile,' said Sleepy. 'The sheriff will be back in an hour or so, I reckon.'

Swede craned his neck and looked across the street toward the Prong Horn Saloon.

'T'ank you,' he said. 'Ay t'ink Ay need some yin.'

He rode his mule over to the saloon and tied the lop-eared animal to the hitch-rack.

'Somebody stole his horse to use as a hearse,' remarked Hashknife.

'What do *you* think?' asked Sleepy.

'I think he needs some gin,' replied Hashknife dryly.

Hashknife was right—Swede did need some gin. In fact, it required six drinks before Swede calmed down long enough to find the sheriff and put in his complaint.

'Yore horse,' explained the sheriff, 'was found in the hills by Smoky Day and the dude. Lon Porter, dead as a nail, was roped to the saddle.'

'Yudas priest!' exclaimed Swede. He was drunk enough to act. 'You say my hurse vars—are you yokin', Sheriff?'

'I'm not jokin', Swede. Lon Porter was tied to the saddle.'

'Ay vill be dorned!' exclaimed Swede. 'Who killed Lon?'

'He never left his name,' said Mañana. 'Mebbe he wasn't proud of it.'

'Maybe you can help us, Swede,' suggested the sheriff.

'Ha-a-a?' queried Swede blankly.

'Where was yore horse when you missed him first?'

'Ay don't know, Sheriff; Ay vars lookin' for him, too.'

'I mean—where was he stolen from?'

'Oh.' Swede squinted thoughtfully. 'Ay vars fixin' fence. Ay tied my hurse at a corner of de fence, because de fence vars in de brosh, and

Ay vent along by hand. Ay vars fixin' fence—'

'Did you hear the shot that killed Lon Porter?'

'Did Ay?—Ay am not sure. Ay t'ink Ay heard a shot. Ay vars hammerin' staples, and—vell, Ay came back and my hurse vars gone. Ay said to myself, Svede, somebody has—'

'All right, that's enough.'

'T'ank yu, Sheriff.'

'You didn't see anybody else, Swede?' asked Mañana.

'Ay didn't even see de man who stole my hurse.'

'You smell like a sawmill,' said Mañana.

'Ay like yin.'

'Takes all kinds of people to make Arizona,' said Mañana.

In spite of the fact that Dean Harder had been shot as a bank robber, it was the biggest funeral ever held in Lost Horse Valley. Everybody in the Valley knew Dean—and liked him. Why he turned to a life of crime was only a conjecture. Many blamed Flint Harder, because of his hard nature and his refusal to help Dean in any way.

They had all felt the wrath of Flint Harder, and none of them felt the least sorrow for him. In fact, no one spoke to him as he entered the room and sat down near the center, instead of going up to the mourners' bench.

Every hitch-rack in town was crowded with horses. The little church was entirely inadequate, so the funeral was held in the dance-hall. Long before the services were due to start, men stood around and talked about Dean Harder. Hashknife and Sleepy heard them talking, and not one said a word about Dean being wrong.

Mañana joined Hashknife and Sleepy near the entrance to the dance-hall stairway, and watched the folks file inside.

'The two men who rode with Dean Harder will be there,' Mañana told them.

'And,' added Hashknife, 'they might be the last two men you'd ever suspect.'

'Ain't that the truth? Man, I wish I knew who they are. Here comes the sheriff. He said that this is the hardest job he ever had to do.'

'I can believe that,' agreed Hashknife.

Jim Martin walked past them and entered the hall.

'Never even spoke,' marveled Mañana. 'Mebbe he'd rather not talk. Old Jim is salt of the earth, and this deal has just about killed him. I'll sure be glad when this funeral is over; and I didn't have any hand in makin' it. I wonder how Flint Harder feels.'

'Worse than Martin—if that's possible,' said Hashknife.

Bob Reynolds, owner of the Rocking R, who had been pointed out to Hashknife, was sitting just across a narrow aisle, and with him was a huge flat-faced man, with big hairy hands. The service started, but Hashknife's mind was too busy to pay attention to the cow-town minister's words. He was trying to identify this big man, trying to remember back to a place and a name.

Mrs. Harder, bowed with grief, was near the casket, but to Hashknife the real mourners were farther back in the room—Flint Harder and Jim Martin. They had everything to regret. The minister droned on interminably, and the organist played off-key, but the huge flat-faced man beside Bob Reynolds never shifted his gaze from the minister.

Finally it was over. Hashknife found Mañana outside, and as Reynolds and the big man came out, Hashknife asked about the man.

'That's Mike Lassen, foreman of the Rockin' R,' said Mañana.

Lassen! Something clicked in Hashknife's mind. Mike Lassen. Hashknife and Sleepy were not going to the cemetery. They sat down in front of the hotel and watched the procession form. Sally Harder rode with Mrs. Harder and Mrs. Long. Bob Reynolds and Mike Lassen mounted near the hotel, and Hashknife asked Sleepy to take a good look at the big man.

'Something familiar about him, but I can't place him,' said Sleepy.

The funeral procession got under way. Hashknife slumped in his chair, his eyes thoughtful.

'What about the big man?' queried Sleepy.

'Sleepy, it was about five years ago. One night we stopped at a Ranger headquarters down on the Rio. They had picked up five rustlers after a gun battle, and they were askin' 'em questions when we came in. Remember?'

'Yeah, I remember that night. Why—I seem to remember somethin' about some of that bunch gettin' away from the Rangers. Three, wasn't it?'

Hashknife nodded slowly. 'I believe it was.'

'Wait a minute!' exclaimed Sleepy. 'There was a big hairy—'

'Larsen,' said Hashknife.

'That's the one! Larsen. They couldn't make him talk. Man, you've got a memory. What do they call him here?'

'Mike Lassen. He's foreman for the Rockin' R.'

'Lovely dove! Foreman, eh? And there's rustlin' bein' done here.'

Hashknife nodded slowly. 'So they say, Sleepy.'

Sleepy sighed and began rolling a cigarette. 'But,' he said, 'we must remember that all we came here for was to find Henry Webster.'

'I almost forgot about Henry. We'll have to talk with Flint Harder. I hope he can tell us somethin' about Henry, so we can get out of here.'

'You don't hope anythin' of the kind, Hashknife; I know you.'

They had been together a long time, these two drifting cowboys, and Sleepy knew that Hashknife would never agree to leaving Lost Horse

75

Valley until he had proved a few things for his own satisfaction. There was no doubt in Sleepy's mind that the telegram from Bob Marsh was only a ruse to get them into the thick of things. And there was no doubt in his mind that Bob Marsh's own detectives had failed. Marsh had wired them to perform an ordinary piece of business, well knowing that Hashknife, once in Lost Horse Valley and aware of the troubled conditions of that range, would never leave until everything was peaceful again.

Sleepy Stevens analyzed nothing. The surface showings were good enough for Sleepy, who left the digging of details to Hashknife. They did not demand remuneration for their services. They needed little. Home was where they hung their hats, and their destination was somewhere on the other side of a hill. Someone had called them Soldiers of Fortune, but Sleepy declared they were Cowpunchers of Disaster, and that Fortune had nothing to do with them. They never bragged of their exploits, nor did they even want thanks.

They had not been long in Antelope Flats before Sleepy realized how cleverly Bob Marsh had played his cards. A bank robbery, cattle-rustling, troubled ranges and troubled people—plus Henry Webster. Sleepy could tell by the glint in Hashknife's gray eyes that he was gathering and discarding theories, even before he knew any of the people.

Few men ever looked into Hashknife's eyes and forgot them. Level, and steel-gray, they seemed to look deep into a man's soul, searching for the truth. Hot-headed gunmen had looked into his eyes, and forgotten to draw. But they could be kindly eyes, too, full of humanity and understanding.

Hashknife lighted a cigarette and said quietly, 'There's tall hills out east of here, Sleepy—when we find Henry Webster.'

'Yeah—when we find him,' yawned Sleepy.

CHAPTER V

A LEFT UPPERCUT
AGAIN PROVES USEFUL

ALEXANDER HAMILTON MONTGOMERY was hardly able to walk next day, but he told Artemus to saddle the horses.

Artemus said, 'Are yuh sure the heat ain't got yuh?'

'It ain't,' replied Montgomery flatly.

'Learnin' fast,' grinned Artemus. 'Well, it's yore joints—not mine.'

The young man had difficulty in getting his left foot up as far as the stirrup, but he gritted his teeth and climbed aboard, adjusting himself gingerly, an expression of pain on his face.

'Where to?' asked Artemus curiously.

'To the Flint Harder ranch, Artemus.'

'To the—my Gawd! All right, all right. I know she's pretty and all that, but Old Man Day's little son Artemus has got everythin' to lose and nothin' t' gain. Flint Harder don't like me. Said I'd have been hung long ago if the seat of my pants was heavy enough to break my neck. I'd hate to be one of them burnt-offerin's they speak about in the Bible.'

'You have nothing to do with my going out there,' said Montgomery.

'Yeah, I know that; and I hope you'll explain it to Flint Harder before he goes into action.'

'My goodness, Artemus! One would think that Mr. Harder was an ogre.'

'Well, I dunno what that is, but it's all right with me. C'mon.'

They rode slowly. Even a slow trot was misery for Montgomery.

'Yore real trouble started at birth,' said Artemus soberly.

'In what way?' queried Montgomery.

'Bein' born with yore knees too close together. When I was six years old I was the width of a good horse between m' knees. I ain't bow-legged. I'm jist built for ridin' a horse.'

'Well, I am not,' declared Montgomery grimly.

'You'll be all right in a coupla years. It takes practice.'

In spite of the fact that the Quarter-Circle H was the biggest spread in Lost Horse Valley, there was nothing pretentious about the group of buildings, hidden away in a grove of huge sycamores. The bunkhouse and part of the ranch-house were of adobe, and there was a thick adobe wall around the spacious patio. The ranch-house was two stories high, roofed with homemade tiles.

Alexander Hamilton Montgomery and Artemus

Day rode up close to the patio gate. Sally Harder, sitting on a rear balcony overlooking the patio, saw them. Flint Harder was asleep in the main room. Wong, the old Chinese cook and house-keeper, saw them and came to the patio porch.

Nick Higby, the foreman, also saw them, and came up from the stable.

'Who you like see?' asked Wong.

'Will you please tell Mr. Harder that a couple of gentlemen are here to see him?' requested Montgomery.

'Make it one gentleman,' said Artemus. 'I jist came along.'

Nick Higby came up to them, evidently in bad humor. He said, 'What are you doin' here, Day?'

'I—I just came,' said Artemus lamely.

'I see yuh did. What do you fellows want, any-way?'

'I should like to see Mr. Harder, if you do not mind,' said Montgomery.

'Just suppose Mr. Harder don't want to see yuh,' suggested Nick.

'That,' replied Montgomery firmly, 'is up to Mr. Harder.'

'Is that so?' queried Nick. 'Mr. Harder don't want to see yuh.'

Alexander Hamilton Montgomery dismounted painfully, and Artemus looked upon such action with trepidation.

'If you do not mind,' said Montgomery, 'I

81

should like to leave that decision to Mr. Harder, rather than to take an opinion from a hired man.'

Sally moved a little closer to the railing of the balcony. She knew Artemus Day very well. He gave her an appealing glance, but his too-large hat slid over his eyes. Nick Higby moved in close to Montgomery.

'Listen to me, you damn fool dude,' gritted Higby, 'I'm foreman of this outfit, and when I tell yuh that Mr. Harder don't want to see yuh . . .'

'I beg your pardon,' said Montgomery, 'but is it customary for the foreman to do the thinking for the owner?'

Nick Higby closed his jaw tightly for a moment. Then he turned and said to Artemus, 'Smoky, take this damn fool off this ranch, before somethin' happens to both of yuh.'

Smoky shoved his hat back, shrugged his shoulders, and the hat went back over his eyes.

Higby turned back to Montgomery and said, 'Get back on that horse and get off this ranch, before I lose my temper and poke you right in the nose.'

'I really cannot conceive of any reason why—'

'You asked for it,' said Nick, 'and you'll get it.' Nick Higby was a one-punch fighter. That is, he threw everything he had into that one punch—and missed. It left him off balance, one fist in the air, as though saluting someone. Alexander Hamilton Montgomery did not miss. It was the same punch that felled Buck Shell at Isabella—a left-handed uppercut to the chin. Nick Higby landed on his face in the dirt. Wong looked blandly upon the affair, while Artemus Day chuckled hollowly. Sally's eyes were watching Montgomery, and she did not seem angry over Nick's downfall.

'Well,' remarked Montgomery, 'now that the argument is over, may we see Mr. Harder?'

'Missa Ha'dah sleep now,' explained Wong. 'Plitty soon he wake up. You wait?'

'Thank you—yes, we will wait.'

Alexander Hamilton Montgomery lifted his eyes and saw Sally on the balcony. 'I beg your pardon,' he said quietly. 'I—I didn't know you were there.'

'Come into the patio,' she said.

He left his horse and walked through the gate. Nick Higby sat up, shaking his head, goggling at Artemus, probably wondering what hit him. Sally came down to the patio before Nick was able to get to his feet. He heard their voices in the patio, but everything seemed very confusing.

Artemus said, 'Yore chin will be sore a coupla days, Nick.'

'Where did he go?' asked Nick huskily.

Artemus jerked a thumb toward the patio. 'He's talkin' with Sally. She saw it from that balcony up there.'

'Oh!' Nick caressed his chin and stretched his neck muscles. Then he turned and walked back toward the stable, not too steadily. Artemus grinned widely and began rolling a cigarette, but first he hung his hat on the saddle-horn.

Sally and Montgomery were sitting on a long bench, and Montgomery was telling her all about why he came West and what he expected to do.

'I can understand all that,' said Sally, 'but why do you want to see my father?'

'As a matter of fact,' confessed Montgomery, 'I wanted to meet you, so I used your father as an excuse.'

'But why go to all that trouble in order to meet me?' she asked.

'It wasn't any trouble, Miss Harder.'

'Fighting is no trouble for you, I suppose.'

'Fighting? Oh, you mean—out there. Well, it really wasn't any trouble.'

'You are accustomed to fighting, I suppose.'

'Not at all. In fact, I have only hit two men in my life.'

'Mr. Montgomery,' said Sally quietly, 'you are quite a remarkable young man, and I appreciate your efforts in getting a chance to meet me; but I am afraid it has gained you very little.'

'I'm sorry,' said the young man. 'At least I have met you, and I think you are wonderful, no matter what you think of me. I want you to know I am sorry about your brother. You see, I was in the bank—at the time.'

'You saw my brother?' asked Sally quietly.

'I saw three masked men, Miss Harder. I admit that I was frightened and excited, but I did note their general physical make-ups. Was your brother left-handed?'

'No, he was not,' declared Sally quickly. 'Why do you ask that?'

'The one man who could have been your brother carried a gun in his left hand, Miss Harder.'

'Are you sure of that?' she asked anxiously.

'Sure of what?' growled Flint Harder's voice, and they turned to see him in the doorway.

Sally said, 'Dad, I want you to meet Mr. Montgomery.'

'That damned dude again,' muttered Flint Harder. 'I didn't believe it when Wong said that you knocked out Nick Higby.'

'I am sorry, Mr. Harder; he struck first.'

'Sorry? You poor fool, he's whipped every man he ever fought!'

'Except one, Dad,' said Sally.

'That fight prob'ly ain't finished yet,' growled Harder. 'What do you want out here?'

'Well,' faltered Montgomery, 'I—I just came out, you see.'

'I see yuh did. Well, yuh can turn right around and go back again.'

'Wait a moment, Dad,' said Sally. 'Mr. Montgomery was in the bank when—when it was robbed. He says that the one man who could

85

have been Dean held his gun in his left hand.'

'Of all the damn—' spluttered Flint Harder, but suddenly sobered. 'What was that?' he asked. 'Held a gun in his left hand?'

Montgomery nodded. 'Your son was under six feet tall, they say. Only one of the three was under six feet tall, and he held a gun in his left hand.'

Flint Harder scowled thoughtfully at Montgomery.

'You wouldn't know,' he said huskily. 'You'd be too scared. Yo're just sayin' that. The evidence—'

'Two gentlemen come see you, Missa Ha'dah,' called Wong from the doorway.

'Tell 'em to go to hell,' replied Harder.

'Tell 'em yourself,' said Hashknife, and they saw him in the patio gateway, with Sleepy behind him.

'Come in,' growled Harder. 'Wait a minute— we'll go into the house.'

They went in through a side doorway, and Harder led the way to the main room. Sleepy was chuckling, and Harder turned on him.

'What's so damn funny?' he asked.

'That dude out in the patio.'

'Oh! That *thing!* Dude, eh? Well, he knocked Nick Higby cold a few minutes ago. Wong told he hit Higby with a left uppercut. Can yuh imagine that?'

86

'Did you ever hear of Buck Shell, down at Isabella?' asked Sleepy.

'Yeah, I've seen him.'

'Well, the dude knocked him out with one punch.'

'He did, eh? Huh! Well, what do you two want of me?'

'We're lookin' for Henry Webster,' replied Hashknife.

'Henry Webster? What do yuh want him for?'

'Do you know who Bob Marsh is?'

'Yeah, I know him.'

'He sent us a telegram at Isabella, askin' us to come up here and locate Henry Webster. Bob wants Webster to get in touch with him.'

Flint Harder scowled at Hashknife and said: 'Why should I do anythin' for Bob Marsh? Twice I've asked him for help to find out who is stealin' my cattle. Did he help me? He did not. If that's all I mean to the Association, I'm through.'

'But that don't locate Henry Webster,' reminded Hashknife.

'Oh, that smart-Aleck! He came out here and said he wanted to investigate all my cows for disease. All it would cost would be his board and room for two-three weeks. I told him my cows didn't have any disease. He said they did. Anyway, we had an argument, and I told him to go to hell. He went back to Antelope Flats, and I never saw him again.'

87

'He never came back, eh?'

'I told him I'd shoot his topknot off if he ever did. The idea! He was just a smart *hombre* who wanted to experiment on my cows.'

'I see,' nodded Hashknife. 'How long after yore request from Bob Marsh did Webster come here?'

'How long? Oh, maybe two-three weeks, I reckon.'

'Harder,' said Hashknife seriously, 'did it ever occur to you that Henry Webster might have been a range detective, sent here by Marsh?'

'No. If he was, why in hell did he want to investigate my cows?'

'Did you ever stop to consider that a rustler shoots to kill, and that a man known as a detective would have no chance to find out anythin'—and maybe not live twenty-four hours?'

Flint Harder eyed Hashknife closely for a moment as he considered the question. Then he said: 'Who in hell are you—askin' all these questions? I know yore name's Hartley—but what's yore business?'

'Punchin' cows,' replied Hashknife soberly.

'Is that so? You don't happen to be another pair of Henry Websters, do yuh?'

'Yore cows can all die of the croup as far as we're concerned,' said Sleepy.

'We've heard,' said Hashknife, 'that the Rockin' R claim to have lost cattle the same as you have.'

'I don't care what happens to the Rockin' R. I'm not interested.'

'Do you get any pleasure out of life, Mr. Harder?' asked Hashknife.

'Pleasure? That's none of your business. I live as I please.'

'Without a friend,' added Hashknife.

'Who says I haven't any friends?'

'Have yuh?'

Harder glared at Hashknife, but turned away.

'What is a friend?' he asked bluntly.

'My idea of a friend,' replied Hashknife, 'is a person who knows all about yuh—and still likes yuh.'

'That's my idea of a gullible damn fool, Hartley.'

'They're nice to have around when things go wrong, Harder.'

'When things go wrong?'

'Like yesterday,' said Hashknife. 'Did any man or woman come to you and say they were sorry? No, they sat away from yuh. They didn't want a tongue-lashin', so they kept away. You got bitter over an accident, and you've nursed that bitterness until yuh can't speak decently to any man. You're just stubborn enough to go to yore grave cussin' everythin' and everybody; but all the while, Harder, yo're wishin' you could change and—have a friend.'

'Yo're a liar, Hartley. Yore whole idea is wrong.'

'Much obliged for the information on Henry Webster,' said Hashknife.

They walked to the doorway, with Harder glaring at them.

'It's shore nice to have met yuh,' said Sleepy.

Flint Harder limped over to a window and watched them ride away. Wong came from the kitchen and stood in the doorway. Harder saw him and limped back to his chair, but without any usual outburst of profanity.

'Yo' like bake spud fo' suppah?' asked Wong.

'Baked spuds?' queried Harder. 'I believe I would, Wong.'

Wong walked back into his kitchen and stopped beside the stove. He rubbed the back of his neck and looked back toward the main room. Finally he shook his head. 'No good,' he told the pots and pans. 'Boss man plitty damn sick today, I t'ink.'

Alexander Hamilton Montgomery and Artemus were riding away as Hashknife and Sleepy came out of the house. Sally was beside the patio gate. She introduced herself to them.

'After all,' she smiled, 'Dad didn't bite either of you.'

'He barked a coupla times,' smiled Sleepy.

Sally laughed. 'He always does.'

'Did he bark at Alexander Hamilton Montgomery?'

'He really didn't have time. Do you know that young man?'

Hashknife explained how they met him and what happened in Isabella.

'It must be habit with him,' said Sally. 'He knocked Nick Higby down just before you came here today. I didn't exactly blame him, because Nick was just a little too officious.'

'He's learnin' the West,' smiled Sleepy.

'Yes—with Smoky Day teaching him. He calls Smoky Artemus.'

'They're a queer pair,' smiled Hashknife. 'Montgomery says he is gatherin' material to make into a play.'

'Yes, he told me that,' said Sally. 'You see, I have had two years at California. I asked him the name of his alma mater, and he said there were three of them—step-alma maters. He said that in no case did he stay long enough to get acquainted with the old ladies.'

'I don't reckon he'd get along very well with yore father,' said Sleepy.

'I am afraid not, Mr. Stevens; Dad is set in his ways.'

'Yeah, he has his likes and dislikes,' smiled Hashknife. 'What sort of a fellow was Lon Porter?'

'Lon was a nice fellow, Mr. Hartley; we all liked him. I can't imagine who killed him. Everything seems to go wrong for us.'

91

'Too much hate,' said Hashknife.

Sally looked curiously at him. 'Hate?' she queried.

'Yeah. Yore father, Jim Martin, and those connected with them.'

'I see what you mean. But I'm afraid it will never be any different. Dad will never change. He hates Jim Martin worse than ever—now. Sometimes he almost hates me for going out to see Nell—Dean's wife. But I always have, and he knows it, but we never discuss it together. He knows I can be just as stubborn as he. Maybe it is in the Harder blood.'

'Maybe it is just yore idea of fair play, Miss Harder.'

'I wish Dad thought so.'

'Maybe he does,' suggested Hashknife.

Sally shook her head. 'You don't know him the way I do, Mr. Hartley.'

Hashknife smiled at her and picked up his reins. 'You can learn a man like him in a short time,' he said.

'Come out again,' she said. 'If you can stand Dad's bark.'

'Thank yuh—and we can,' laughed Hashknife, as they rode away.

As they rode back to Antelope Flats, Sleepy said: 'What did I tell yuh about Bob Marsh? All he wanted was for us to find Henry Webster and tell him to write. Bob knew there was trouble here. He sent Henry here, and somethin' happened to Henry. So Bob Marsh, the schemer, figured we'd shy from the job if he told us the truth; so he asked us to pack a message to a man who wasn't here. He knew darn well that as soon as yore long nose poked into things here, nothin' short of dynamite would pry yuh loose.'

'I'm still lookin' for Henry Webster,' said Hashknife meekly.

'Knowin' we won't find him,' added Sleepy.

They stabled their horses and were on their way to the hotel when two riders drew up at the Prong Horn Saloon.

'We seem to have an old friend among us,' observed Sleepy.

'That's right,' smiled Hashknife. 'Slim Sherrod, ridin' with Mike Lassen, who used to be Larsen. A good pair to draw to, Sleepy. Yuh know, I believe I'll send a telegram to Bob Marsh tonight. I'd like to know somethin'.'

'What's that?' queried Sleepy.

'I want to know if Henry Webster was ever a member of the Rangers.'

CHAPTER VI

A. H. MONTGOMERY WANTS TO FIND A LEFT-HANDED MAN

DANNY LONG sat on the porch of his little ranch-house with his wife, and talked over the troubles of the Harder family,

'I don't know what Nell will do,' said Mrs. Long. 'Dean had no money to leave her. The price of beef is down, and even if it wasn't, she hasn't anything to market. Jim Martin has only his salary—and you know how they stand. She wouldn't accept a dime from him.'

'Flint Harder could help her,' suggested Danny.

'Could you imagine that, Danny?'

'No, I couldn't, May.'

From down at the stable came the sounds of a man singing—or trying to sing. It was not very musical. Danny shook his head sadly.

'Swede brought more gin from town,' he said. 'I can't figure him out. He was only good for one drunk a year—unless he met Alphabet Anderson at a bar. But he's been drunk practically day and night since Dean was killed. Somethin' is wrong with him.'

'If he keeps this up, you'll have to fire him, Danny,' said Mrs. Long.

'Fire Swede? Gosh, May, I can't do that—unless I have to. Aw, he'll sober up. Why, he'd do anything short of murder for either of us—and I wouldn't bet he'd balk at murder.'

Swede led his horse out of the stable and started to saddle. Swede's horse was fifteen years old, swaybacked, with a motheaten buckskin coat, and barely enough energy to break into a lope. Just now Swede was having difficulty in saddling the animal, because of Swede's inebriated condition, not because of the horse.

'He's prob'ly goin' to forget the cinch,' chuckled Danny. 'One day the saddle is plumb over the withers, and the next day it's on the rump. But it's all the same to Swede. He says he's an all-around rider.'

'What is he waving at?' queried Mrs. Long.

Danny chuckled. 'He's waving at me, I reckon. I'll go down and see what he wants.'

Swede was in the saddle when Danny came up to him.

'Didja want somethin', Swede?' asked Danny.

'Ay vant to tell you somet'ing,' said Swede heavily. 'Ay can only stand it yust so long.'

'Stand what?' asked Danny curiously. 'Gin?'

'Yin be damned!' snorted Swede. 'Ay vould do anyt'ing for you, Danny. Ay t'ink you are de greatest faller in de vorld, but Ay get all yittery inside.'

'Bad gin,' suggested Danny. 'But what do you want to tell me?'

Swede leaned down from his saddle, his face red from the exertion. 'Ay yust vant to tell you next time you kill a man—bury him yourself. Ay am t'rough vit bein' undertaker.'

Swede spurred his ancient steed and went galloping toward the main gate, leaving Danny staring after him, puzzled completely. Danny went up to the house and sat down on the steps of the porch.

'What did he want, Danny?' asked Mrs. Long.

'I think he's gone crazy,' said Danny. 'He told me that if I killed another man I must bury him myself, because he is through bein' an undertaker.'

'Well, my goodness!' exclaimed Mrs. Long. 'He must be crazy, Danny.'

'I suspect bad gin,' sighed Danny.

'He didn't say who you killed, did he?'

'No, he didn't mention any names,' laughed Danny.

'It really is queer, Danny. Swede never acted crazy before.'

'No,' replied Danny soberly, 'he never did. May, I believe I'll go to town and see what I can hear. You never can tell what Swede might tell—if he has gone loco. And if he is crazy, we don't want him around here, that's a cinch. Yeah, I believe I'll ride in.'

· · ·

Swede Olson came to town and headed straight
for the Prong Horn Saloon, where he proceeded
to drink one glass of gin after another, until
even the bartender looked at him in amazement.
Hashknife and Sleepy were in the saloon, and
their attention was attracted to the big Swede.

'Somethin' is wrong with the big fellow,' whispered Hashknife. 'He's tryin' to drown himself in
gin.'

'He works for Danny Long,' said Sleepy. 'Look
at that old cap-and-ball six-gun he's packin'.'

Hashknife smiled and watched Swede, who
finally turned and walked with uncertain steps
toward the doorway. The bartender shook his
head as Swede stumbled out on the sidewalk.

'Darn near a quart,' said the bartender.
'Whooee-e-e, what a thirst!'

Swede stood on the sidewalk, adjusted his old
sombrero, pointed a finger toward the sheriff's
office, as though charting his course, and went
into the street. Hashknife and Sleepy, together
with several other men, went to the doorway to
watch Swede cross the street.

But Swede had his bearings and went straight
to the open door of the office, where he stumbled
over the threshold and nearly fell inside. The
other men went back, but Hashknife and Sleepy
went outside. Danny Long rode in and tied his
horse at the hitch-rack in front of the general

store. Then he came across to the saloon. He nodded to Hashknife and Sleepy as he went in. A few moments later, they could hear the bartender telling Danny about Swede's drinking bout. Then Danny came out, a puzzled expression on his face.

'Did you see that Swede drinkin' gin?' he asked.

'Yeah,' grinned Sleepy. 'What's wrong with him?'

'Well, he's sure actin' funny,' replied Danny. 'I dunno—'

Jim Martin, the sheriff, came from his office, and looked toward the saloon for several moments before coming across the street.

Danny said, 'Is Swede over at yore office?'

'Yeah, he's over there,' replied the sheriff. 'Danny, I—I'm sorry as the devil, but I've got to arrest yuh.'

Danny jerked back. 'Arrest me?' he gasped. 'What for, Jim?'

'Swede has charged you with the murder of Lon Porter.'

'Lon Porter? Martin, are you jokin'?'

'I wish I was. Swede says you killed Porter and hid the body in a manger. Swede says he took the body away to hide it, but when he met two men he got scared and ran away. He says his conscience wouldn't let him keep still any longer.'

'But I never shot Lon Porter,' insisted Danny. 'That drunken Swede—'

'Danny, I want yuh to go peacefully,' said the sheriff. 'Maybe Swede is crazy—I dunno. But I've got to arrest yuh.'

'I'm not goin' off half-cocked,' said Danny grimly. 'I'll go with yuh. But that Swede is both drunk and crazy, Jim.'

'I hope so, Danny. C'mon.'

Hashknife and Sleepy tried to talk with Swede, but he was too drunk to do anything except wave his arms dismally. Some strong coffee and an hour of sleep put him back on his feet. He was repentant, but stuck doggedly to his story.

'But why would Danny Long shoot Lon Porter?' asked the sheriff.

'Ay am not figure for a reason,' sighed Swede. 'Ay am so sorry, but Ay could not sleep. Ay am honest faller, you bat you.'

'Loyal to the core,' sighed Mañana.

'You read that in a book,' said Sleepy.

'How'd yuh know that?'

'I read it myself, Mañana. It's a good thing to say about an apple.'

Hashknife went to the jail and the sheriff let him talk with Danny, who was sitting disconsolately on a bunk smoking a cigarette. He looked up as Hashknife came to the bars.

'What do you want?' asked Danny curiously.

'How about a little talk?' queried Hashknife, leaning against the bars. 'The sheriff didn't ask yuh many questions.'

'I reckon he believed Swede,' replied Danny soberly.

'What did Swede tell him?'

'You know as much about it as I do. Swede's drunk—and crazy, too. Too much gin. Before he left the ranch he told me that next time I killed a man I'd have to bury him myself. He said he was tired of bein' an undertaker. I tell yuh, he's gin-crazy.'

'But the fact still remains that he did try to bury Lon Porter's body.'

'That's got me puzzled,' admitted Danny, scowling at the floor.

'Did you ever have any trouble with Lon Porter?' asked Hashknife.

'Not trouble. I didn't like any of Harder's outfit, but I wouldn't shoot one of 'em—unless I had to. I never shot Lon Porter. Swede says he found the body in a manger in my stable. Would I be damn fool enough to hide a dead man in my own stable?'

'You didn't see Lon Porter that day, did yuh, Danny?' asked Hashknife.

'I haven't seen him for a week. Swede told the sheriff that he saw me at home that day and a little later he heard the shot. When he came to the ranch, I was gone. Then he found Lon's body in the manger.'

'He heard the shot, eh? Did you hear any shot?'

101

'I fired that shot myself—at a crow. But would anybody believe that?'

'Did yuh hit the crow?' asked Hashknife.

'I shot his tail off,' smiled Danny. 'I'd hate to be hung by the tail of a crow.'

The absence of Doctor Jessup had delayed the inquest over Lon Porter, but he came back that day. Hashknife and Sleepy went down to see him, and found the sheriff, Mañana, and Nick Higby there. Doctor Jessup was about sixty-five years of age, nervous and irritable. He seemed to resent Hashknife's questions.

'How long had he been dead when they brought him here?' he snapped. 'How do I know? I never heard the shot.'

'Was he shot in the back?' asked Hashknife meekly.

'If he was, what difference does that make? They hang 'em down here, no matter which side they're shot from.'

'Guilty or not,' said Hashknife dryly.

'What do yuh mean by that?' asked the sheriff.

'All they need is the word of a drunk who heard the shot.'

'He wasn't drunk at that time, Hartley.'

'That might make his hearing more acute,' said Hashknife.

'What did he mean by that?' asked the sheriff, after they left the house.

No one seemed to know. Nick Higby said, 'What's he hornin' in for?'

'Don't look at me,' protested Mañana. 'At least he's smart enough to ask questions. Did yuh ever look him square in the eyes?'

'What for?' asked the sheriff.

'You'll have to answer that one, Jim,' said Mañana. 'Try it some day when he asks yuh a question, and yo're tryin' to think of a good lie.'

'Will that give yuh the right answer?' asked Higby.

'It sure will, Nick; and yore answer will be the truth.'

'Yo're crazy,' growled the sheriff.

'Yeah, and I'm just as happy as though I had good sense.'

Hashknife and Sleepy went back to the hotel, where Andy Vincent gave Hashknife a telegram from Bob Marsh. It read:

HENRY WEBSTER WAS MEMBER TEXAS RANGERS TWO YEARS. LOCATE HIM IF POSSIBLE. REGARDS TO SLEEPY.

'Regards to Sleepy!' snorted Sleepy. 'That's sarcasm. Locate him if possible! He knew darn well we couldn't locate him. I wouldn't trust Bob Marsh as far as I could—'

'Throw a bull by the tail,' finished Hashknife.

103

'Uh-huh. A Hereford bull—and by the tail, Hashknife.'

'Yeah. One of them big white-faced ones, with kinky hair on his face and a white rim around his eyes. Yuh can hear him at sundown, pokin' down a ridge, singin', "I'm go-o-o-oin' ho-o-o-ome, I'm go-o-oin' ho-o-ome." I know the kind yuh mean. Pretty heavy to throw by the tail.'

'Thank yuh very much, Mr. Hartley.'

'Yo're welcome, Mr. Stevens.'

'And now,' said Sleepy, 'all we've got to do is to find Henry Webster, who used to be a Texas Ranger, and who only stayed here long enough to meet Flint Harder.'

'And possibly Saint Peter,' added Hashknife.

'Do yuh think somebody killed him?'

'They either did or they scared him so badly that he ain't quit runnin' long enough to write to Bob Marsh.'

'I wish somebody would do that to us,' sighed Sleepy.

Artemus Day came across from the Prong Horn Saloon, grinned wryly, and sat down with them.

'Where's yore pupil?' asked Sleepy.

'A. H. Montgomery,' replied Artemus dryly, 'is up in his room, ponderin'.'

'Ponderin' what?'

'I dunno. Ever since he talked with Sally Harder, he's been kinda trance-like. He hired me for a hundred a month and my board and room to

104

learn him. Now I've got a new job—lookin' for a left-handed man.'

'What kind of a left-handed man?' asked Hashknife.

'He didn't say.'

'Have yuh found any yet?' asked Sleepy.

'Not yet.'

'Didn't he say why he wanted a left-handed man?' asked Hashknife.

'No, he just said he wanted to find out where there was one. If yuh see one, let me know, will yuh?'

'Do yuh want us to hold him for yuh?' asked Sleepy.

'He said all he wanted was the man's name.'

'You're right-handed, ain't yuh?' asked Sleepy.

'I sure am.'

'I can see his object,' said Sleepy dryly. 'He's got a right-handed teacher, and now he wants a left-handed teacher, so he can learn both sides of the question.'

'Sure,' grinned Artemus. 'I never thought of that. Maybe I better go up and see how he's comin' along in his ponderin'.'

Hashknife squinted thoughtfully over his cigarette after Artemus had gone into the hotel. Why was Montgomery looking for a left-handed man? he wondered. Artemus had said that after talking with Sally Harder, Montgomery had asked him to locate a left-handed man. Why?

Flint Harder came to town in his buckboard, driven by one of his cowboys. Harder saw Hashknife and Sleepy and ordered the cowboy to take the team over there. The cowboy tied the team and left Harder in the buckboard. Hashknife and Sleepy nodded to him, but paid no further attention to him.

Finally Harder said, 'Hartley, would yuh mind comin' out here?'

Hashknife walked out and climbed up beside Harder, who said, 'The whole damn town will be wonderin' what we're talkin' about.'

'A little serious thought wouldn't hurt any of them,' said Hashknife.

'I believe yo're right.'

Hashknife laughed. 'They say you never agree with anybody.'

'I don't care what they say. I got a letter from Bob Marsh.'

'About Henry Webster?'

'No—about you.'

'Oh!' said Hashknife quietly. 'Go ahead.'

'Does Bob Marsh always tell the truth, Hartley?'

'Does any man—always?'

'I never met one that did. But if he told half the truth, I can use you.'

'Harder, I don't know what he wrote. Me and Sleepy came here to locate Henry Webster for Bob Marsh. We can't do that, it seems, so we might as well drift along.'

106

'I saw Henry Webster once, maybe two months ago. But I'm not interested in Henry Webster. As I said, I can use you two.'

'Yo're only short one man,' said Hashknife. 'Danny Long is in jail, charged with killin' him.'

'Danny Long? I didn't know that. How come?'

Hashknife explained about Swede's confession.

'That'll hang Danny Long, Hartley,' he declared.

'He hasn't been convicted yet, Harder.'

'He will be. Lost Horse Valley don't like murderers.'

'Don't Lost Horse Valley believe in justice?'

'Maybe. I believe in an eye for an eye, Hartley.'

'Unless it happens to be *your* eye, Harder.'

Flint Harder turned his head and looked at Hashknife. For a moment their eyes met, and Harder turned away.

'I reckon we're all like that,' he said. 'The other feller don't mean much to me.'

'That's what *you* think, Harder. But down in yore heart—'

'Never mind my heart! Don't preach about my heart. Damn it—'

'There's no use of us arguin',' smiled Hashknife. 'I'll drop off here.'

'Wait a minute, Hartley. Bob Marsh says you're

the only man to handle this rustlin' case. My son was shot for robbin' a bank, and a friend of my son is in jail for killin' one of my best men. You can't help my son, and I don't care a damn about Danny Long, but I do want this rustlin' to stop. Will you take the job?'

'To save yore cows, eh?' said Hashknife slowly. 'That's all that means anythin' to you, Harder. You don't care if Danny Long swings, and you don't care what they say about your son. You hate Jim Martin. You admit that the Rockin' R has lost cattle, but you say to hell with them. And you ask me and my pardner to risk our lives to save *your* cows.'

'Then yuh won't take the job, eh?'

'When a man is as mean and narrow-minded as you are, Harder,' said Hashknife, 'he don't deserve help. Why, I could almost shake hands with the rustler who stole your cows.'

Hashknife got out of the buckboard and sat down with Sleepy, who had heard some of the conversation. Flint Harder hunched on the buckboard seat until the cowboy came back across the street.

Harder said, 'We're goin' home, Pete.'

They drove away. Harder never looked toward Hashknife and Sleepy.

'You made a smart decision,' said Sleepy.

'I made a smart talk,' smiled Hashknife.

'What do yuh mean, pardner?'

'Flint Harder won't spread the word that we're workin' for him.'

'Uh-huh. Yuh don't suspect *his* gang, do yuh, Hashknife?'

'I don't want a bullet in the back from *anybody,* Sleepy.'

Montgomery and Artemus came from the hotel and sat down with them.

'I hear yo're lookin' for a left-handed cowboy,' remarked Sleepy.

Alexander Hamilton Montgomery laughed. 'I'm not making an issue out of it,' he said. 'I—I just wondered if there were any left-handed cowboys. You see, in the story I intend to write, I want details correct.'

'Uh-huh,' grunted Sleepy, satisfied with the explanation. But Hashknife was not convinced by such an explanation. He studied the tenderfoot, wondering just what was the real reason.

'How is that story comin' along?' asked Hashknife.

'Oh, it hasn't started. You see, I want to study characters, study the country, get all my facts correct. I must have characters, outlaws, heroes, and all that—and a pretty girl.'

'You've found her, ain't yuh?' smiled Hashknife.

Alexander Hamilton Montgomery smiled slowly.

'I—I hope so,' he confessed. 'But her father is not exactly cordial.'

'That old vinegaroon!' snorted Artemus.

'Artemus!'

'Oh, all right. But I can think what I damn please.'

'Think, but do not express,' said Montgomery.

'All right. He's bullied and bluffed everybody for a long time, but he don't bluff me—and he knows it. That's why he growls ever' time I come near him. If he ever monkeys with me, I'll jist about rent his earthly envelope. Sally is fine, but that old *pelicano*—I don't like him.'

'Artemus!' warned Montgomery.

'Where in the devil didja get that name?' asked Sleepy.

'From Ma and Pa,' said Artemus. 'I never thought anybody'd find it out, but the time I met Mr. Montgomery I was drunk. Somethin' made me tell him my real name—and now look at me.'

'I like it,' said Montgomery.

'Yo're the only one,' said Artemus. 'Pa said he got it out of a book. They was deadlocked for a week over my name. Pa wanted to call me Alcibiades, but Ma hung on for Artemus. It didn't make no difference which one won—I lost.'

'Yore folks had ideas, too, Monty,' said Sleepy soberly.

'Yes,' agreed Montgomery, 'I'm afraid they did. Especially for a country like this. Monty is all right; it fits in around here.'

'Names,' said Hashknife, 'don't mean any-thing.'

'No?' queried Sleepy. 'Suppose they had called you Charlemagne.'

'We ain't goin' to dwell on the possibilities,' laughed Hashknife.

CHAPTER VII

A LOT OF BROKEN GLASS

'AY AM hort-sick and sad,' declared Swede Olson from the witness stand at the inquest. 'But Ay am honest man and Ay had to tell.'

Swede was practically sober. Everybody in Lost Horse Valley came to the inquest. Danny Long's wife sat with him, and only a few seats away was Mrs. Dean Harder. Alexander Hamilton Montgomery and Artemus were there to testify, but Swede Olson was the man in the spotlight. No one questioned nor disputed Swede's testimony until Doctor Jessup excused him, when Hashknife stood up and asked the coroner for the right to question Swede.

'The man has told his story,' said the doctor. 'I can't see—'

'That's the whole trouble—you don't even try,' said Hashknife.

'Let him ask a question, Doc,' said the sheriff. 'It can't hurt.'

'All right,' growled the doctor. 'I still don't see—'

Hashknife interrupted him with the question, 'Mr. Olson, you say you heard the shot that killed Lon Porter?'

'Ay t'ink it vars de shot, because—'

'You just *think* it was,' said Hashknife. 'Was your horse tied in that stall when you took him out that day?'

Swede squinted thoughtfully. 'No, he vars not. My horse vars in de corral.'

'Was Danny Long's horse tied in that stall all that night?'

'No, he vars not. Both horses vars in de corral.'

'Mr. Olson,' smiled Hashknife, 'how long since a horse was fed in that stall?'

'Ay don't know. May be t'ree-four days.'

'As a matter of fact, Mr. Olson, that body could have been there two days before you found it.'

'By Yudas, das is right!'

'That's all, Mr. Olson. Thank you, Doctor.'

'But what have you proved?' asked Doctor Jessup.

'I have proved that Danny Long could have shot at the crow as he has testified.'

The room buzzed with conversation. All eyes were upon the tall, grave-faced cowboy, who had gained an important point for Danny Long.

Alexander Hamilton Montgomery and Artemus were put on the stand, but their testimony made little difference. After a short conference, the six-man jury asked that Danny Long be bound over to the Superior Court and tried for the murder of Lon Porter.

Mrs. Long and Mrs. Dean Harder waited

outside for Hashknife, and Mañana Higgins introduced them.

Mrs. Long asked, 'Are you a lawyer, Mr. Hartley?'

'Mrs. Long,' smiled Hashknife, 'do I look like a lawyer?'

'You talk like one; and you have helped Danny.'

'I didn't like Swede's testimony,' said Hashknife. 'I believe he is honest, of course, but it was mostly his imagination.'

'People around here are liable to believe anything,' said Mrs. Harder.

'People are like that everywhere,' said Hashknife. 'Lost Horse Valley is no exception, Mrs. Harder. I wish you would have a talk with your father. After all, yo're his daughter. Why, a pleasant word from you would make a new man of him.'

'He's aged twenty years,' sighed Mañana.

'I—I don't believe he wants to talk with me,' said Mrs. Harder.

'Don't you believe it,' said Hashknife quickly. 'You try it, ma'am.'

Hashknife and Sleepy went over to the Prong Horn Saloon, where a crowd of men were discussing the inquest. Hashknife realized that his questioning of Swede Olson would cause plenty of comment. Slim Sherrod and Mike Lassen, foreman of the Rocking R, were at the bar, and Sherrod was saying:

'Yeah, he likes to shoot off his face. Me and him was with the UF outfit together. Some folks might think he was smart, but personally, I think he is just an ignorant, long-legged puncher who can't keep his mouth shut.'

There was no buzz of comment over this statement, and Slim Sherrod realized it. He turned his head slightly and saw Hashknife and Sleepy.

The crowd watched quietly. Slim's right foot slipped off the bar-rail, and his spur jingled loudly.

Hashknife said, 'Keep on talkin', Slim; you sound interestin.'

Slim jerked around, feigning amazement at seeing Hashknife. 'Oh, hello, Hartley!' he exclaimed. 'Well! Do yuh like this country better than the Isabella Range?'

'Any country is all right,' replied Hashknife. 'It's the people that ruin it.'

'Yeah, that's right,' agreed the embarrassed Slim. 'I—I'm with the Rockin' R now. I'd like to have yuh meet Mike Lassen, the foreman.'

Lassen said, 'Hyah,' but with little enthusiasm.

The pause was embarrassing. Slim tried to grin, shrugged his shoulders, and said, 'Well, how are yuh, anyway?'

Hashknife did not reply. Slim said, 'Hello, Sleepy; I didn't see yuh.'

'I'm kinda transparent,' said Sleepy quietly. 'At times yuh have to look real close to see me at all.'

116

'Slim,' said Hashknife quietly, 'you didn't happen to be speakin' about me as we came in, did yuh?'

Slim was on the spot. Too many men had heard him for him to make any denial. He said: 'Aw, you know how it is. Yuh say things like that—well, kinda offhanded thataway, and—well, you know—'

'No, I didn't know,' denied Hashknife.

Lassen turned from the bar and faced Hashknife. 'Are you tryin' to start trouble?' he asked harshly.

'Well, I'll be darned!' exclaimed Hashknife. 'Larsen! I thought Slim said Lassen. Last time I seen you was down on the Rio.'

Lassen's jaw sagged for a moment, but he regained his nerve quickly. 'The name is Lassen,' he said. 'I never seen you before in my life.'

Hashknife ignored him, and turned to Slim Sherrod.

'What became of Les Hart?' he asked.

'Les Hart? Why, he—'

Lassen shoved Slim aside and faced Hashknife. Lassen's right hand was tensed above the butt of his holstered gun.

'My name's Lassen, Hartley,' he said huskily. 'Do yuh understand that?'

It was a tense moment, and there was not a sound in the saloon. Then a front window sprayed glass, and the glasses and bottles along the back bar erupted in a shower of glass. Hashknife ducked and Mike Lassen dived straight ahead, right across the shoulder of Hashknife, who heaved up, throwing Lassen over his shoulder, and the big foreman of the Rocking R landed on his head and shoulders on the floor.

It seemed that everyone was diving for cover. A card table upset and a shower of poker-chips rattled across the floor. Strangely enough the report of the shot was so muffled that few even heard it. But there had been plenty of havoc along the back bar, and the bartender was flat on the floor, trying to reach up and dislodge a sawed-off shotgun from an upper shelf of the bar.

'Where did that come from?' asked an awe-struck gambler. No one knew.

Mike Lassen was trying to pump air back into his aching lungs. Hashknife leaned against the bar, a twisted smile on his lips, as he kept an eye on Lassen. The bartender got up gingerly and looked at his wrecked back bar. Several bottles of bonded stuff had fairly exploded their contents all over the place, and there was a long crack across the mirror.

Mike Lassen tried to draw his gun and managed to get it out of his holster, but Sleepy kicked it out of his hand and it slid under a table.

'Yuh can't depend on anybody nowadays,' said Sleepy calmly.

Hashknife and Sleepy walked outside and the

crowd followed them. Artemus Day was coming across from the hotel, walking slowly. He stopped near the sidewalk, where he cuffed his hat back and looked at the crowd.

'Mr. Montgomery asked me to apologize,' he said slowly. 'Yuh see, he—he was practicin', and he thought his sixshooter would stay cocked—but it didn't.'

'Up in his room?' asked Sleepy.

'Uh-huh—with the window open.'

'That damn fool dude!' exploded the sheriff. 'That gun won't never stay cocked.'

'He knows it,' said Artemus blandly.

The crowd went back into the saloon, but Hashknife and Sleepy walked back to the hotel with Artemus.

'Yuh see,' explained Artemus, 'Mr. Montgomery owns a pair of glasses that are so strong that yuh can see a fly on a stable a mile away. From our window we can look square into the Prong Horn Saloon.'

'Meanin' which?' asked Sleepy.

'Well, yuh see, that Mike Lassen is awful fast with a gun.'

'He is, eh?' queried Hashknife.

'Uh-huh. I was a-lookin' through the glasses, personally, and it kinda—well—'

Hashknife smiled slowly. 'And you saw us about to lock horns, eh?'

'Well, I—I kinda thought—yuh see, if a man's

119

attention is attracted to somethin' else, he might kinda forget—'

'In other words,' said Hashknife, 'it was yore gun—not Montgomery's.'

'Yore guess is as good as any,' grinned Artemus. 'I don't like him either—and I didn't know how fast you are with a gun.'

'I sure appreciate that, Artemus,' said Hashknife soberly. 'Yo're all right, pardner.'

'It wasn't anythin',' depreciated Artemus. 'I shore sent them-there glasses a-hellin', didn't I? First fun I've had since I turned valet to a damn dude.'

'You didn't find that left-handed man, did yuh?' asked Sleepy.

'No, I ain't yet. Well, I'll have to go back and tell the boss that everythin' is all right. See yuh later.'

'Much obliged, Artemus,' said Hashknife. 'If we meet a left-handed man, we'll let yuh know.'

'Thank yuh very much.'

'You've got a guardian angel, Hashknife,' chuckled Sleepy.

'I may need one before this deal is over,' replied Hashknife soberly.

CHAPTER VIII

HASHKNIFE FINDS HENRY WEBSTER

HASHKNIFE and Sleepy rode out to Danny Long's ranch next day. Swede Olson was working at the corral, and came out to meet them.

'Are you workin' here?' asked Hashknife.

'Yeh,' nodded Swede. 'Ay told Mrs. Long Ay had to do somet'ing to pay her back. Ay feel awful bad about Danny.'

'After all, Swede, you did the right thing.'

'Ay am honest, but Ay am also a damn fule.'

'One balances the other,' smiled Hashknife.

Mrs. Harder was with Mrs. Long, and they came out on the porch.

'I was in town early to see Danny,' said Mrs. Long. 'There will not be a term of court for over a month. Danny was very grateful to you for your questions at the inquest, and he wants to talk with you.'

'I'll see him,' said Hashknife. 'So Swede came back to work, eh?'

'I couldn't pay him anything, but he insisted on working. He blames himself for all our trouble.'

Hashknife turned to Mrs. Harder. 'I'd like to ask a few questions about yore husband,' he said quietly. 'I know it must be painful, but I—'

'What can be talked about?' she asked bitterly.

'Oh, a few things. I don't need to ask you if Dean needed money.'

'He did need money,' she said. 'Who doesn't? But he wouldn't rob a bank. His father wouldn't give us a cent, and my father—don't you understand? He and Flint Harder hated each other. When Dean and I ran away and got married, they both disowned us. I think they hated each other worse than ever after that. I can't go back to my dad and ask for help.'

'You don't hate your dad, do yuh?' asked Hashknife.

Tears came into her eyes and she turned away.

'All right,' said Hashknife. 'He may hate Flint Harder, but he don't hate you. I believe he'd help yuh if yuh asked him.'

The two women were silent for a while, and then Mrs. Long said, 'Nell, why don't you tell him what happened?'

'It was in the mail today,' said Mrs. Harder. 'Two hundred dollars, and nothing to show who sent it. It had been mailed at Antelope Flats.'

'That was sure nice,' said Hashknife.

'Do you suppose my father sent it?'

'You will have to make yore own guesses, Mrs. Harder.'

Hashknife questioned her on Dean's actions at home on the day of the bank robbery,

'Dean went away early that day,' she said. 'He

122

was depressed over money, and he said he was going to see his father. The last thing he said was, "Honey, he can't any more than throw me off the ranch." '

'Did he go to the ranch and see his father?'

'No, he didn't. I asked Nick Higby, and he said that Dean did not come to the ranch that day.'

'Here comes the dude and his valet,' said Sleepy.

Mrs. Long laughed. 'Mañana Higgins told me this morning that the dude almost wrecked the Prong Horn Saloon yesterday when his gun went off accidentally in the hotel and the bullet came into the saloon.'

'What is he doing in this country?' asked Mrs. Harder.

'Ma'am,' said Hashknife, 'the answer ain't in the book.'

Alexander Hamilton Montgomery and Artemus rode up to the porch. The two women knew Artemus, except that they called him Smoky. He introduced them to Montgomery.

'We were just riding around,' said Montgomery. 'I find it very exhilarating, since I am getting used to the saddle.'

'I heard that you are a writer,' said Mrs. Long.

'Still in embryo,' smiled Montgomery.

'He means,' explained Artemus, 'he ain't hatched yet.'

'Artemus!' exclaimed Montgomery.

'Well, that's how yuh explained it to me.'

'I suppose it is all right, except that it makes me sort of an egg.'

Hashknife laughed and got to his feet. 'I believe we will go back to town. I'll drop in and see Danny, Mrs. Long.'

'Thank you—he will be very glad to see you both.'

'If you don't mind,' said Montgomery, 'we will ride back with you.'

'The more the merrier,' grinned Sleepy.

'Is it possible to cut across the hills to town?' asked Hashknife.

Mrs. Long went to the corner of the porch and pointed across the hills. 'Go around the stable and across the dry-wash, and you will find a trail which leads to the canyon. It is a deep canyon, but not very long. If you circle the head of it you will strike another trail, which will take you direct to Antelope Flats. Danny used to go that way most of the time.'

'I know the trail,' said Artemus. 'Been over it lots of times.'

'It will be an adventure for me,' said Montgomery. 'I have never been off a street or a traveled road in my life.'

They found the old trail beyond the dry-wash, where they strung out in single file, with Artemus leading the way, until they reached the rim of the canyon. The canyon was about two hundred feet wide at that point, and about a hundred feet deep.

They drew up on the rim and let their horses rest. Cattle grazed on the opposite rim. Somewhere a quail lookout for a covey, sent his call echoing across the canyon. A cottontail came down among the rocks, but froze at the sight of the four riders.

'Simply gorgeous!' exclaimed Montgomery. 'I had no idea.'

'Yeah, it's pretty,' agreed Sleepy, and reached down to scratch a match on his boot-sole.

Possibly that sudden action saved his life. As he leaned down, a bullet slit a hole in the crown of his sombrero, tore through a fold of Montgomery's shirt, and smashed up on a rock behind them. Sleepy merely let loose and landed on the ground. Hashknife and Artemus were out of their saddles in a flash, yelling at Montgomery to get down. He did—ungracefully, but well— and Hashknife fairly shoved him flat.

'Hurt, pardner?' asked Hashknife quickly.

'Skinned knee,' replied Sleepy. 'Ventilated my hat, too.'

Another bullet whined off the rock behind them.

Hashknife said, 'They're usin' rifles; we better hunt a hole.'

'What is it?' asked Montgomery anxiously.

'It ain't an accident,' replied Artemus, as another bullet screamed off a rock.

'But I do not understand,' protested Montgomery. 'We haven't done anything.'

'They don't know it,' said Sleepy dryly. 'C'mon, we'll get into that crevice. It'll give us a chance to use our guns if they come close.'

Another bullet threw rock dust into Sleepy's eyes, and he swore angrily as he slid into the crevice. Artemus was alternately lifting and ducking, a cocked revolver in his right hand.

'Hold still, you darned sandpiper!' snapped Sleepy. 'Keep yore head down, will yuh?'

'We've got to get lower,' said Hashknife calmly. 'They can circle the top of this crevice and blast us out with their rifles.'

'You can't!' wailed Artemus. 'You'd fall into the canyon.'

'Take a look, Sleepy,' said Hashknife.

Sleepy went crawling down the crevice, while Hashknife kept watch. Montgomery was thoroughly frightened. Someone was trying to get through some brush above a pile of rocks. Two more shots hummed off the rim of their crevice, showing that the attackers were getting almost high enough to rake their position.

'Them dad-burned dry-gulchers!' complained Artemus, and ducked when a bullet almost parted his hair.

Hashknife got a glimpse of one of the men. He had reached the spot in the rocks, but was blocked by some heavy brush. The man started to part it with his gun-barrel, when Hashknife lifted his sixshooter and squeezed the trigger. There was a convulsive movement in the brush and the clang of metal on stone as a rifle fell among the rocks.

Sleepy was calling, 'C'mon down here—it's a cinch!'

'Get down there,' ordered Hashknife. 'I'll hold 'em back.'

Montgomery and Artemus scuttled down the crevice. Hashknife saw a bush wiggling, and smashed two bullets through it before he followed. What seemed to be the end of the crevice was a broken ledge, two feet below the rim of the crevice, where a man might crawl to other ledges, protected by an overhang of sandstone. In order to follow up their attack, the attackers would have to expose themselves on that rim, where the six-shooter would have the advantage.

Sleepy was rolling a cigarette, with Montgomery and Artemus close to him.

'Didja hit anythin'?' he asked as Hashknife came over to them.

'I got one of them, Sleepy. At least, he fell in the brush and dropped his rifle.'

'My God!' exclaimed Montgomery. 'You killed a man?'

'They tried to kill us,' replied Hashknife calmly. 'If yuh don't believe it, take a look at the hole in yore shirt.'

'I know—but it is terrible, just the same.'

'Do yuh wish yuh was safe at home?' asked Sleepy.

'I—well—come to think of it—no.'

'Salty as a codfish,' said Artemus. 'Yo're learnin'.'

Hashknife sniffed audibly. 'Do you smell anythin'?' he asked.

'Buzzards,' said Sleepy. 'Must be a roostin'-place near here.'

'Might be. I just wonder—'

'Wonder what?' asked Sleepy.

'You watch the end of that crevice,' said Hashknife. 'I'm goin' to take a look.'

Hashknife worked his way past them on the ledge and crawled farther along under the rocky overhang, where there was a sort of cave. There he stopped and studied an object. It was hardly more than the skeleton of a man, with most of the clothing torn away. Buzzards had made identification impossible. As Hashknife examined the remains, several more rifle shots echoed back from the canyon walls.

Hashknife crawled quickly back to the others, who were intently watching the crevice. In a few moments they heard a voice calling, 'Which way did they go, Mañana?'

'Around the rim of the canyon, Jim!' yelled Mañana Higgins.

Hashknife scrambled up the crevice again, with

the others following. The sheriff and deputy were near there, watching the rim of the canyon, both men armed with rifles. They jerked around at sight of Hashknife and the others.

'I'm damned!' snorted Mañana. 'Like four gophers!'

'Who was doin' all the shootin'?' asked the sheriff.

'I only saw one of 'em,' replied Hashknife.

'How many did you fellers see?' asked Sleepy.

'I saw two of 'em, goin' like hell,' said Mañana.

'There were three different rifles,' said Hashknife, 'which makes me a pretty fair shot. C'mon.'

Hashknife led the way up through the brush where he had seen the man—and the man was still there, sprawled across a rock, his rifle below him. The sheriff shoved through the brush and dragged the man out.

'Les Hart!' he exclaimed. 'That's who it is— Les Hart.'

'Do yuh know him, Hashknife?' asked Mañana.

'He was with the UF,' said Hashknife, 'and he was Slim Sherrod's bunkie.'

'Why would he try to kill you?' asked the sheriff curiously.

'I wish I knew the answer to that one,' replied Hashknife. 'How did you two happen along?'

'We heard the shootin' from the road,' replied the sheriff, 'so we came to find out. They took a couple shots at us, too. But why would they be waitin' here for you fellers?'

'Very simple,' replied Hashknife. 'They were staked out along the road, with one of 'em watchin' Long's ranch-house. When we cut through the hills they tried to cut us off. There's somethin' else I want to show yuh, Sheriff. The rest of yuh stay here.'

Hashknife took the sheriff down to the skeleton, while the rest of them watched for signs of the other two men.

'Was you and the sheriff goin' out to Long's place?' asked Sleepy.

'Yeah,' drawled Mañana. 'Danny said he needed some clean clothes, so we rode out to get 'em.'

'My regards to a dirty shirt,' said Sleepy soberly.

Hashknife and the sheriff came back, bringing a piece of cloth from the suit the man on the canyon shelf had worn. It was dirty and torn, but that was their only hope of identification.

They roped the body of Les Hart on the sheriff's saddle, and he and Mañana rode double to Antelope Flats, where their coming created quite a sensation. No one seemed to know that Les Hart had come back to the Valley. The crowd followed down to the doctor's house, but Hashknife saw Flint Harder in his buckboard and went over to him.

130

'Who's the corpse?' asked Harder gruffly.

'Les Hart,' replied Hashknife.

'Les Hart? Why—when did he come back here?'

'I don't know, Harder.'

'Shot?'

'Yeah. Him and a couple more men were tryin' to kill us over at the canyon between here and the Long ranch. I got Hart.'

'Why were they shootin' at you, Hartley?'

'Yuh can't get an answer from a dead man—and the other two got away. Harder, I wonder if you can remember how Henry Webster was dressed.'

'Dressed? Huh! I don't remember. Store clothes, I reckon.'

Hashknife spread the piece of dirty cloth on his knee, and Harder looked at it closely.

'I believe he wore that kind of a suit,' said Harder. 'Kinda green and gray, mixed. Yeah, I remember it now.'

'And he wore shoes instead of boots?'

'That's right—shoes.'

'Henry Webster,' said Hashknife, 'was shot between the eyes, and cached away on a ledge in that canyon between here and Danny Long's ranch.'

Flint Harder eased his crippled hip to a more comfortable position.

'How did you happen to find him?' he asked.

131

Hashknife explained about the attack at the canyon, and how he found the remains. Harder listened, his lips set in a grim line.

'So Webster *was* a range detective,' he muttered. 'Somebody knew him. But I don't figure out Les Hart.'

'Hart and Sherrod were both with us on the UF,' said Hashknife. 'They were still there when we left the outfit at Isabella, and they both knew that we were comin' up here.'

Flint Harder nodded slowly. 'Now that you've found Henry Webster—are yuh leavin' the Valley?'

'I suppose we'll drift along pretty soon, Harder.'

Flint Harder took a folded piece of yellow paper from his pocket and handed it to Hashknife. It was a telegram to Harder from Bob Marsh, and it said:

LEAVE EVERYTHING TO HARTLEY

Hashknife gave the telegram back to Harder, his face grave. 'Has anybody else read that?' he asked.

'Only me and Nick Higby.'

'Do you trust Nick Higby?' asked Hashknife.

'Trust him?' Harder swore feelingly. 'Certainly I trust him. He's my foreman. What are yuh drivin' at, Hartley?'

'Just this,' replied Hashknife quietly. 'You are losin' cattle and the Rockin' R are losin' cattle. One range detective has been murdered. Today I had to kill a dry-gulcher who used to work for you. Is it any wonder I ask who you can trust?'

'Well, you can trust Nick Higby.'

'Harder,' said Hashknife, 'you've seen that motto on a dollar. It says, "In God We Trust." Well, I'll go further and say I trust my pardner. But the cemeteries are full of men who trusted.'

'All right,' growled Harder. 'Who gives a damn who you trust or don't trust?'

'I do, Harder.'

'I don't suppose you'd even trust me.'

'Not an inch—when my life depended on it.'

'Much obliged,' said Harder dryly. 'I appreciate that.'

Hashknife started away, but went back to Harder. 'Hang on to yore temper,' he said, 'because I'm goin' to ask yuh a question, and I want an honest answer.'

'You said you wouldn't trust me an inch,' reminded Harder.

Their eyes met for a moment, and Hashknife said, 'I expect an honest answer, Harder.'

'Go ahead,' growled Harder.

'On the day yore son was killed, did he come to the ranch askin' you for money?'

'That's none of yore business. Why do yuh ask?'

'I need the correct answer, Harder.'

The old cattleman's face hardened and he was about to refuse to answer, but Hashknife said, 'What time did he come out there that day?'

'I don't know what time it was. It—' Harder stopped and drew a deep breath. 'Tricked me, eh? All right, damn yuh, he did come. I don't know what time it was. I never carry a watch, and that damn Wong busted my clock. I was asleep when he came, so I don't know what time it was.'

'Was Nick Higby at the ranch when Dean came?'

'Higby? What's he got to do with it? Suppose he was—what then? Are you tryin' to drag Nick Higby into somethin'?'

'Much obliged,' said Hashknife.

'To hell with you and yore questions,' growled Harder, as Hashknife walked away.

Hashknife smiled to himself. If Nick Higby *was* there, he lied when he told Dean Harder's wife that Dean never came there that day. Why would Higby lie about a thing like that? he wondered.

Nick Higby came back to the buckboard, and Harder told him he was ready to go home. Nick had seen Harder talking with Hartley. He mentioned it to Harder, who made no comment.

'You heard about Les Hart?' asked Higby.

'Yeah, I heard about him. Prob'ly got what was comin' to him.'

'If yuh believe everythin' yuh hear,' said Higby.

'Why not? Les was no damn good.'

'Maybe not—I dunno.'

There was no more conversation on the way to the ranch, and Harder even seemed to forget to swear at Higby when he helped him out at the ranch-house. Sally met her father in the main room, but he waved her aside as he hobbled to his chair.

'Did you see Mr. Hartley?' she asked.

'Yes, I saw him,' growled Harder.

'He wouldn't take the job?'

'He would not. Said he didn't trust me.'

'Didn't trust you, Dad?'

'Well,' growled Harder, 'after all—why should he? Today he killed Les Hart.'

'He killed Les Hart?' asked Sally, in amazement.

Flint Harder nodded soberly. 'Hart and two other men tried to kill Hartley and his pardner. Two of them got away. Smoky Day and that damn dude were with Hartley.'

'But why would Les Hart try to kill Hartley?'

'I don't know. And Hartley found the body of Henry Webster, the man who wanted to work out here—to test my cows for diseases.'

'I remember him,' said Sally. 'But why was he killed, Dad?'

'He was a cattle detective.'

'Oh! And Mr. Hartley refused to help you?'

'He did. The best detective in the West—if you

believe Bob Marsh. Hartley don't like me—and I don't like him.'

'Are they going to stay in Antelope Flats?' asked Sally.

'Prob'ly not. They came here to find Henry Webster. Well—they found what was left of him today. Hartley says that after what has happened around here, he don't trust anybody—not even me. Damn it, I don't blame him. I don't trust anybody—not even Hartley; so we're even.'

'I might talk with Mr. Hartley,' suggested Sally.

'You keep away from him. I'm not askin' any woman to help me—not even my own daughter. Hartley's slick. He tricked me today. Asked me if Dean came out here to borrow money from me the day that bank was held up. Asked me what time he came, and like a damn fool, I said I never carry a watch—and the clock was busted.'

'But what difference did that make?' asked Sally. 'What if Dean did come out here that day, Dad?'

'I don't know—he didn't say. And he asked if Nick Higby was here at the time. I don't know why he wanted to know that. I accused him of tryin' to drag Nick into it, and he laughed at me. Damn him, when he laughs at yuh—with his lips—'

'With his lips?' queried Sally, puzzled.

'And his eyes don't laugh,' said Harder. 'You figure it out; I think I'll take a nap.'

CHAPTER IX

A. H. MONTGOMERY FINDS A LEFT-HANDED MAN

WHEN the sheriff and the coroner went out to get the remains of the skeleton at the canyon, they brought back Les Hart's horse. It was the same horse Les had ridden with the UF outfit, and was branded with a Circle JR on its left shoulder. Hashknife asked Mañana about that brand, and was told that it was located about a hundred miles east of Antelope Flats and in another county.

'It belongs to Jack Rett,' said Mañana. 'That's a wide country over there, and the spreads are far apart. They have to drive about twenty-five miles to a sidin' on the railroad. They tell me that Rett has a fair-sized outfit.'

'Is there a road from here?' asked Hashknife.

'No road, but yuh can go through the hills. Yuh can make it easy in two days.'

Hashknife and Sleepy went down to the little depot, where Hashknife wired Bob Marsh:

THINK WE LOCATED HENRY WEBSTER BUT THE BUZZARDS GOT

THERE FIRST. WIRE DISPOSITION OF
REMAINS TO SHERIFF THIS TOWN.

'Is your name Hartley?' asked the sleepy-eyed
agent.

Hashknife nodded and the agent handed him a
telegram from Bob Marsh, which read:

IMPORTANT YOU SEE BOB
REYNOLDS. REGARDS TO SLEEPY.

Sleepy snorted in disgust.

'Sendin' me his darned regards! He makes me
tired. I wouldn't trust him as far as I could throw
a white-faced bull by the tail.'

The agent laughed, and Sleepy looked tri-
umphantly at Hashknife. 'I knew I'd make
somebody laugh—some day,' he said.

'I wasn't laughin',' denied the agent. 'It's a
nervous disorder.'

'What are yuh goin' to do about that telegram?'
asked Sleepy, as they walked back from the
depot.

'Ain't we goin' out to meet Mr. Reynolds?'

'Nope. Early in the mornin', we're goin' ridin',
Sleepy.'

'Yeah? Any special place?'

'No—just ridin', Sleepy.'

'Uh—huh. How'd it be if we ask the sheriff for
a couple rifles to take ridin' with us?'

'They might come in handy, pardner. I want to have a little talk with Danny Long, too. We might pick up a snack of food at the restaurant to take along.'

'Just a innocent little picnic, eh?' smiled Sleepy.

'Looks innocent from here,' replied Hashknife, 'but yuh never can tell—from here.'

When Flint Harder ate supper with his cowboys there was rarely any more conversation than needed. It only required a spark to send Harder into a conflagration. Tonight he seemed more grim than usual. He had been talking with Nick Higby, and Nick admitted the loss of more cattle.

As Wong piled smoking dishes on the table, Harder said: 'For the last time, I'm tellin' you boys that this rustlin' has got to stop. If it don't, I'll fire every damn one of yuh and get a new crew.'

Flint Harder glared around the table and waited for this to sink in. None of the cowboys looked at him. Finally he said, 'I reckon yuh all know that Hartley killed Les Hart, when Hart and two other men was tryin' to kill Hartley.'

'That's what Hartley *says,*' remarked Pete Soboba.

'There's no question about what happened,' said Harder. 'What in hell was Les Hart doin' here?'

No one seemed to know the answer.

139

Higby said, 'I saw Slim Sherrod from the Rockin' R, and he said he hadn't seen Les since he left the UF.'

'Sherrod,' said Harder, 'would lie when a truth would serve him better. Now, I want yuh all to understand this. About two months ago a man who said his name was Henry Webster came out here. He claimed to be a veterinary. He wasn't— he was an Association detective, sent here at my request. I didn't know it. Today, Hartley found the remains of Henry Webster on a ledge of the canyon over by Long's ranch. The man had been shot through the head and left for the buzzards. There was enough of his clothes left for me to identify him.'

'That's the man Hartley and Stevens were lookin' for,' said Higby.

'That's what they say,' nodded Harder. 'I got a telegram from the Association sayin' that Hartley is better than any man they've got. I asked Hartley to take this job, and he told me to go to hell.'

'I've heard about Hashknife Hartley,' said Bill Nichols. 'I was with the SK spread, over in New Mexico, and one of the boys mentioned that Hashknife Hartley was in town. Next mornin' we was two men short.'

'*Mucho malo hombre*, eh?' queried Pete.

'They tell me,' replied Nichols, 'that he don't just use his head to wear a hat on.'

'He don't *look* bad,' smiled Higby.

'Neither does dynamite, Nick. I ain't never met the gent, but when I do I'm sure goin' to be *mucho amigo* with him, y'betcha.'

'Well, this cattle-rustlin' has got to stop,' declared Harder. 'I'm not able to take a gun and ride on their trail. I've got to set here and listen to you fellers prove an alibi. Hartley won't take the job. At least, he is honest. I've taken more off him than off any man I ever met—and liked it. I'm not quittin' on him—not as long as he's in this valley.'

'Maybe he's scared to take the job,' suggested Pete Soboba.

'Yuh think so, do yuh?' rasped Harder. 'I'd like to have yuh meet him and tell *him* that.'

'Hell, I'm not pickin' trouble for myself,' laughed Pete.

'Look what he done to Mike Lassen in the Prong Horn,' said Nichols. 'When that fool tenderfoot smashed a bullet into the back bar. Hartley threw Lassen over his shoulder and damn near killed the big ape.'

'That bullet probably saved Hartley from a bullet in the guts,' said Pete. 'Mike Lassen is awful fast with a gun.'

'Who'd he ever kill?' asked Nichols. 'Ain't nobody ever showed me the list.'

'Anyway, he's fast,' declared Pete.

'Yeah, he prob'ly told yuh that,' said Nichols.

'No use quarrelin',' said Higby.

Wong filled the pot with more steaming mulligan.

Nichols said, 'Maybe Hartley is workin' on the murder of Webster.'

'I don't know,' said Flint Harder. 'He came to me and asked me if Dean came out here to get money from me the day he was shot.'

Higby looked up quickly. 'What'd he ask that for?'

'I don't know. He even wanted to know what time he got here.'

Nichols laughed. 'It was sure funny the way he twisted up Swede Olson at that inquest. He's nobody's fool, that Hartley.'

'He's nosey, that's a cinch,' said Pete.

'I hope he keeps on bein' nosey,' said Harder. 'Maybe if he gets nosey enough, I can save some cows.'

'That's right,' agreed Nick Higby, 'but I never had much faith in a range detective.'

'Hartley ain't a range detective,' said Harder. 'Bob Marsh said he's not workin' for the Association, but that he's smarter than any men they've got on the payroll.'

'What about that damn dude?' laughed Pete.

'Maybe he's a detective,' suggested Nichols. 'I saw Smoky Day today. The dude calls him Artemus. Smoky came to me and asked me if I knew any left-handed punchers in the Valley.

I didn't happen to know any. He said his boss wanted him to find one.'

'A left-handed cowboy?' queried Higby.

'That's what Smoky said, Nick.'

'That's damn funny,' said Flint Harder. 'Why in the devil does he want a *left-handed* cowboy?'

'I don't believe Smoky knows why,' smiled Nichols. 'I can't think of one, can you, Nick?'

'I ain't that interested in the wants of that dude,' growled Higby.

'He might be a detective, at that,' said Nichols soberly.

'Les Hart might have been shootin' at him instead of at Hartley. The dude got a bullet through his shirt, they say, and Sleepy Stevens got one through his hat.'

'I'd believe anythin', after Henry Webster turned out to be one,' said Flint Harder. 'Bill, will you hitch up the buckboard team and take me in town? I want to talk with Hartley.'

'Right away,' replied Bill Nichols.

Artemus 'Smoky' Day leaned against the end of the bar at the Prong Horn Saloon, as nonchalant as a man could be who had a hat several sizes too large. Artemus was still looking for a left-handed cowboy, and Alexander Hamilton Montgomery had told him to stay on the job until he found one. They seemed very scarce around Antelope Flats.

Suddenly Artemus stiffened. Several cowboys

were coming in, their spurs raking across the rough floor as they came up to the bar. Artemus drew a deep breath. One of those cowboys wore his gun on the left side, with the butt to the rear, indicating that the man did not use a cross-draw.

Artemus shoved away from the bar and went across the street, where he hurried upstairs in the hotel. Alexander Hamilton Montgomery was writing a letter when Artemus surged in.

'I've done got yuh a left-hander!' he blurted.

'You have? Good work, Artemus. Show him to me, please.'

They hurried down the stairs and went across the street to the saloon. Through a front window Artemus pointed out his discovery. Montgomery seemed pleased.

'His name's Ed North, and he's from the Rockin' R,' said Artemus.

'Excellent!' exclaimed Montgomery. 'Very, very well done, Artemus.'

'Now,' said Artemus, 'that we've found him, what do I do next?'

'I don't exactly know,' replied Montgomery. 'Wait! Do you know where we may find Mr. Hartley?'

'He's gone,' said Artemus. 'Him and Sleepy rode away an hour ago.'

'And just when I wanted him,' sighed Montgomery. 'I don't—I have it! I shall ride out and see Miss Harder!'

'Uh—huh,' said Artemus. 'I spend two days lookin' for a left-handed cow-waddie, and after I find one—you go courtin'.'

'I am not courting, Artemus,' said Montgomery severely. 'This is serious. I must see her at once. You will stay here.'

'And keep lookin' for another left-handed puncher; so you'll have a set.'

'An excellent idea, Artemus; you have great initiative. Come and help me saddle my horse.'

They went to the stable, where Artemus wanted to teach Montgomery how to saddle his own horse.

'If yuh ever have to do it alone, you've got to know which end of the saddle faces the front,' declared Artemus.

'Artemus,' said Montgomery severely, 'I am in a hurry.'

'Uh-huh.' Artemus carefully smoothed the saddle-blanket. 'In a big hurry, eh? Well, far be it from me to chide yuh, but yo're runnin' yore pants into barb-wire—goin' out there alone.'

Artemus slid the big saddle into place, gave it a shake, and reached for the cinch.

'Now—about that left-handed man,' he remarked. 'Yuh see—'

'He is left-handed, is he not?' asked Montgomery impatiently.

'Must be. Wears his gun on the left side, with the butt facin' the rear.'

'What does that mean?'

'Well, some fellers wear a gun on the left side, but they've got the butt facin' the front. They're cross-fire gents. No, I'd say that North is a natcheral left-hander.'

Artemus put his knee against the horse and yanked the cinch tight. 'But what's the difference—right- or left-handed?' he asked.

'Perhaps,' said Montgomery, 'I am peculiar.'

'Gawd!' breathed Artemus. 'I'd tell a man!'

'But,' added Montgomery, 'as long as you work for me, I expect you to follow my orders and not question my motives. Move aside, while I mount.'

'In the stall?' queried Artemus. 'You better let me lead him out where you've got room. Never mount in the stall unless you want to take a chance on gettin' both legs and yore neck busted. Honest, you better take me along. I'll jist worry myself sick.'

'I . . . don't . . . need . . . you. Is that plain?'

'Severely,' replied Artemus, as he led the horse out of the stall. 'But was you jokin' when you said I'd stay here and look for another left-handed cowboy?'

'I was not joking,' assured Montgomery, 'but I hope you do not find one.'

Artemus helped him mount the horse and watched him ride away in the darkness.

'I'll be dry-nurse to a dinny-sour,' whispered

Artemus. 'Asks me to look—and hopes I don't find one. If that feller don't finish up as a sheepherder, I'll sure miss my guess—or I will.'

Flint Harder and Bill Nichols came to Antelope Flats and Nichols searched for Hashknife, but with no success. He found Mañana Higgins, who told him that Hashknife and Sleepy had left about dark and had borrowed two rifles from the sheriff's office. They had not told anyone where they were going.

Nichols brought this report back to Flint Harder in the buckboard, who swore angrily. 'Borrowed rifles, eh?' he snarled. 'What for?'

'Mañana didn't say, Mr. Harder. I'll see what else I can find out.'

Artemus Day, on his way back from the stable, went past the buckboard, and Flint Harder snapped, 'Smoky!'

Artemus jerked around and came haltingly to the edge of the sidewalk. 'You call me, Mr. Harder?' he asked.

'C'mere, you bowlegged scorpion,' ordered Harder.

'I—I'm close enough,' said Artemus.

'All right. Where did Hartley and his pardner go?'

'I dunno, Mr. Harder; they just went.'

'I see. Where's yore dude?' asked Harder.

'Oh, you mean Mr. Montgomery?'

'Are there any other dudes in Antelope Flats?' queried Harder.

'I don't guess there is. Well, he—he went ridin'.'

'So he went ridin', too, eh? Alone?'

'Yessir,' admitted the harassed Artemus.

'Ain't yuh afraid you'll lose him?'

'No, sir; he knows the road out to yore place.'

'Out to my place? You mean—Smoky, did that—' Harder hesitated.

'I never said he did. I just said he knowed the road out there.'

'Oh, yuh did, eh? Find Bill Nichols for me— right now!'

'I'm workin' for Mr. Montgomery,' said Artemus bravely. 'You hire yore own valets.'

Then the brave Artemus walked into the hotel and went upstairs.

'I sure told him,' muttered Artemus. 'Him orderin' me around thataway! Who does he think he is, anyway? I'm just as good as Flint Harder, any day in the week.'

Artemus yanked open the door and walked inside. Then he stopped short.

Someone shut the door behind him. A voice said, 'Don't move!'

'I—I won't,' declared Artemus.

The barrel of a gun was shoved into his ribs and he shrank back.

'Hold still, you little rat,' rasped a harsh voice. 'Where's the dude?'

'I don't know,' wailed Artemus.

'Yo're a liar, Day! Where's the dude?'

Artemus tried to think up a plausible lie, but the pressure of that gun was too heavy. He said, 'He's gone.' Artemus's voice was so weak it even surprised him. The room was very dark and he couldn't even see the men. But that gun muzzle was no imagination on his part.

'Gone where?' asked a voice. 'If you lie, this gun goes off.'

The man's breath was redolent of liquor, and the pressure of that gun increased until it was making Artemus's ribs sore. Then he heard the click of another gun as it was cocked in the dark. Artemus capitulated.

'He—he went to the Harder ranch,' he said weakly.

'He did, eh?' growled the man. 'What for?'

'I—I dunno why,' gasped Artemus. 'Don't shove on that gun—I ain't goin' to do anythin'.'

'You bet you ain't. Why did he go out there?'

'I told yuh I didn't—'

Artemus's hat was knocked off and a hand grasped him by the hair, giving it a vicious twist. Artemus wore his hair fairly long and the leverage was strong. He yelped.

'One more yelp and you die!' snapped the man. 'Now, the truth, you little sidewinder. What is this talk about him lookin' for a left-handed man?'

'I don't know—honest,' whined Artemus. 'He—he asked me to look for one. I dunno what he wanted him for.'

'Is this dude a detective?'

Artemus wanted to laugh. Alexander Hamilton Montgomery a detective! He tried to frame a good answer, but his hair was at the point of pulling out of his scalp.

A voice said: 'No use askin' him. Take it easy now.'

A hand slid across his face, fingers located his jaw, and a moment later a huge fist drove him across the room, where he bounced off the bed and went to sleep on the floor. A few moments later his door closed quietly. Several men went down the hall and left the hotel by the rear stairway.

Alexander Hamilton Montgomery was not in any great hurry to reach the Harder ranch. One reason was that he wanted time to think things over, and another reason was he didn't want to take any chances of falling off his horse. He realized his limitations.

As he rode slowly in the darkness, he tried to visualize the left-handed man at that holdup. Of course, it might have been that the man had an injured right hand and was holding the gun in his left hand. He had had a good view of Ed North, and he seemed to be about the same build. However, there might be other left-handed cowboys in that country.

Anyway, he was going to tell Sally about Ed North, who was about the same general build as her brother. Alexander Hamilton Montgomery was not at all anxious for anyone else at the Harder ranch to see him, especially the foreman.

He dismounted near the stable and cautiously approached the house. There was no light in the bunkhouse and only a dim light in the main room. He knocked quietly, and after a few moments he heard Sally's voice saying, 'Who is it?'

'It is I—Alexander Hamilton Montgomery,' he replied.

Sally opened the door and admitted him. She glanced past him, expecting to see Artemus Day, and then closed the door. The one lamp burned dimly. Montgomery looked around quickly.

'Did you come alone?' she asked.

He nodded quickly. 'I thought it would be better,' he said.

'Has something happened?' she asked anxiously.

'I think so. Tonight I located a left-handed cowboy.'

'You did? Who was he, Mr. Montgomery?'

'His name is Ed North.'

'Ed North? Yes, I know him. He works for the Rocking R.'

'That is what Artemus told me. I saw him in the saloon, and he answers the description very well.

I hardly know what to do next. We have no proof, you know.'

Sally hesitated, walked back to the table, where she turned up the lamplight.

Montgomery said, 'Is your father at home?'

'No,' replied Sally. 'He went to town. But he wouldn't be of any help, because he wouldn't believe you.'

'That,' said Montgomery sadly, 'has been my misfortune all my life. No one believes me.'

'I believe you, Monty,' said Sally quietly.

'You do? And you called me Monty!'

'It shortens things,' said Sally.

'That is true. But what is our next move?'

'We might see the sheriff and tell him,' suggested Sally.

Montgomery shook his head. 'He wouldn't believe me.'

'We might see Mr. Blair, the prosecuting attorney.'

'I've never met him—and that might help us.'

'Anyway,' smiled Sally, 'we can try him. I'll get my hat. Luckily, my horse is in the stable.'

Sally lighted a lantern and they went down to the stable, where she saddled her own horse. Montgomery wanted to help her, but she was so efficient that he stood back and admired her.

'You know just what to do,' he remarked.

'I should,' she laughed. 'I've done this all my life.'

She tightened the cinch and backed the animal out of the stall.

'You can put out the lantern,' she said. 'Just give it a jerk.'

Montgomery lifted the lantern off the peg, and a voice said, 'Hold still, you tenderfoot.'

Montgomery whirled around. There were several masked men in the doorway of the stable. He hesitated, as the lantern-light glinted on their guns. One of them had grasped Sally by the arm. Montgomery flung the lantern at them and tried to pull his gun, but they came into him with a rush and crashed him back against the wall. Something struck him over the head and he saw stars for a moment.

Then he realized that they were carrying him outside and in a dim sort of way he was aware that they were trying to put him on a horse. He kicked and struck feebly and a man swore bitterly, indicating that even a feeble effort bore fruit.

A man snarled, 'He needs another pettin', I reckon.'

Then he saw more stars and drifted into unconsciousness.

CHAPTER X

ARTEMUS ADDRESSES ENVELOPES

ARTEMUS DAY regained consciousness in that dark room, crawled into the hallway, and got to his feet. The whole episode was clear in his mind, but he had no idea how long he had been knocked out. Nursing his sore jaw and conscious of a lump on the side of his head, he went down the stairs. No one was in the lobby, so he went outside. Flint Harder had finally located Bill Nichols, who was just climbing into the buckboard when Artemus came out. The lights from the hotel windows gave sufficient illumination to show that Artemus was rubbing his head and jaw with both hands.

'What happened to you, Smoky?' asked Bill Nichols.

'Happened?' wailed Artemus. 'Some danged dry-gulchers was in my room and knocked hell out of me in the dark. Wait'll I find them *pelicanos*!'

'Why would they beat you up?' asked Flint Harder.

'How'd I know?' wailed Artemus, clinging to a porch-post. 'Dang 'em, they socked me on the jaw and the head.'

'It don't make sense,' said Bill Nichols.

'What did they want?' asked Flint Harder.

'They wanted Mr. Montgomery. The damn fools said he was a detective, and made me tell where he is. Then they popped me.'

'A detective?' queried Flint Harder. 'Is he a detective, Smoky?'

'No! Yo're as crazy as they are.'

'Made you tell where he is?' queried Nichols. 'Where is he?'

'He's out at Harder's ranch—I think. Anyway, that's where he went.'

'What did he go out there for?' asked Flint Harder anxiously.

'I don't know,' complained Artemus. 'He don't tell me everythin', but,' he added maliciously, 'I think he went to see Sally, if yuh ask me.'

'Yuh do, eh? We'll see about that. All right, Bill.'

Bill Nichols swung the team around in the street and headed for the ranch. In spite of his physical pains, Artemus Day chuckled. Someone stopped beside him and he turned to see Jim Martin, the sheriff.

'What ails yore jaw?' asked the sheriff. 'Tooth-ache?'

'Teeth be damned! Some fellers bushed me in my room and beat hell out of me awhile ago. Take a look at the side of my head! And look at that jaw!'

'Would yuh mind tellin' me why?' asked the sheriff.

'I wouldn't—if I knowed exactly. Yuh see'—Artemus leaned against a post and spat painfully—'this here Alexander Hamilton Montgomery wanted me to find him a left-handed puncher. So I—'

'Why did he want a left-handed puncher, Smoky?'

'Gawd only knows—I don't. I went out to the Harder ranch with him, and he had a talk with Sally. After that, he only had one idea, and that was to find himself a left-handed cowpuncher. Well, I found one tonight. He's Ed North, from the Rockin' R spread. So I told Montgomery, and he got excited. We looked at North through a window, and Montgomery said I'd done fine. Then he decided to go out and see Sally Harder.

'Well, I went up to my room and they grabbed me in the dark. The darn fools wanted to know what I wanted a left-handed puncher for, but I can't tell 'em, 'cause I don't know. They asked me if Montgomery is a detective, and I said he ain't. They ask me where he is, and—and they've got a gun-barrel in my ribs; so I told 'em. Then they socked me, and that's all I know.'

'You didn't recognize any of them, Smoky?'

'No, I don't know who they was.'

'A left-handed cowpuncher,' muttered the sheriff. 'I don't see . . . wait a minute! You was in

157

the bank when that holdup took place. Was there a left-handed one among the three men?'

'Don't ask me, Sheriff; I wasn't watchin' real close.'

'Ed North. Yeah, I know him. He's about the same size as—'

'Montgomery said somethin' about sizes, too. I don't know what he meant.'

'Smoky, I'll bet Montgomery is in for trouble. Get yore horse and meet me here; we've got to go out and see what's goin' on at Harder's ranch.'

'*You* go out to Flint Harder's ranch?' queried Smoky.

'To hell with him—I'm the sheriff. Get yore horse.'

Bill Nichols did not spare the buckboard team going back to the ranch. Everything seemed serene and no one in sight. But Sally was not in the house. Nichols went to the bunkhouse and routed out Nick Higby and Pete Soboba. They did not know that Montgomery had been there.

'Her horse was in the stable,' said Bill Nichols. 'I put him in there today.'

An examination of the stable showed that both her horse and saddle were missing. Flint Harder was both mad and worried.

'Somethin' is wrong,' he declared. 'Sally wouldn't go away with that dude.'

'Where would they go?' wondered Nick Higby.

158

'If they went away, they went awful quiet. Me and Pete played pitch for about an hour before we went to bed, but we never heard a sound.'

Flint Harder sat down in the main room and swore roundly.

'Just wait until I get my hands on Montgomery,' he threatened.

'If they went to town,' said Bill Nichols, 'why didn't we meet 'em?'

No one could answer that. Nick Higby, standing near the door, lifted his head. He could hear the thudding of hoofs as two horses neared the house. The rest of them heard it.

Pete said, 'They're comin' back, I'll bet.'

No one moved. Heavy footsteps came up to the doorway, and Nick Higby said, 'Evenin', Sheriff.'

'Sheriff?' snorted Flint Harder. 'Why, that—'

'Take it easy, Harder,' said Jim Martin, and stepped into the room. Just behind him came Artemus Day. Harder and Martin faced each other.

'Did yuh find Montgomery here?' asked the sheriff.

Grim-faced, Harder shook his head.

Nick Higby said, 'Are yuh sure he came here, Martin?'

'All I know is what Smoky said. He told Smoky he was comin' here.'

'Why did you come out here?' asked Harder huskily.

'Some men beat up Smoky in his room, tryin' to find out where they could locate Montgomery. Why they want him—I dunno. But men don't beat up a man for nothin'. If they wanted Montgomery bad enough to beat up Smoky to find out where Montgomery is—they ain't just wantin' to pass the time of day with him.'

'I'd hate to think so,' said Artemus dryly.

'But why would they want Montgomery?' asked Higby. 'There must be a reason. What did they say to you, Smoky?'

The little bowlegged cowboy rubbed his sore jaw.

'One of 'em,' replied Artemus, 'asked the other to hold still.'

'And then what?' asked Higby.

'Whap!' snorted Artemus, 'and the light went out.'

'I think he's crazy,' said Pete Soboba.

'If I ain't,' replied Artemus, 'I've shore got a constitution like an ox.'

'Where's Sally?' asked the sheriff.

'She's gone,' replied Harder. 'Don't ask me any more—I don't know.'

'Gone? Both of 'em gone? Harder, this is serious.'

'All right—it's serious!' snapped Harder. 'Have yore own way about it. Go on back to town! Git off this place! Damn it, if I need a sheriff, I'll send for one. The rest of yuh get out. Go to

160

Antelope Flats—anywhere. See if yuh can find her. Yo're wastin' time—gawpin' at me.'

'F'r once in yore life, you've got somethin' to cuss about—somethin' real,' said Artemus. 'It must be a relief—after all the cussin' you've wasted on other things.'

Harder leaned forward in his chair and glared at the little cowboy.

'If you don't get out of here in ten seconds,' he said harshly, 'I'll shoot yore damn topknot off, Day!'

'I wouldn't feel it,' said Artemus quietly, but he went out.

Artemus and the sheriff mounted their horses and started back to Antelope Flats.

'What can yuh do with a man like him?' asked the sheriff.

'Nothin' legal,' replied Artemus.

'What do yuh mean, Smoky?'

'It's agin the law to shoot a man jist because he's a damn fool.'

'Might be a good law, too,' said the sheriff dryly. 'He don't like you either.'

'I'm not worryin' about Flint Harder, Sheriff; I want to find Sally and my meal-ticket. I jist can't afford to lose Alexander.'

'They ain't lost—yet,' reminded the sheriff hopefully.

'They've got a damn good start,' commented Smoky. 'Maybe nothin' has happened to them,

161

but them *hombres* who beat me up shore wanted to get their hands on Alexander Hamilton Montgomery awful bad. I know darned well he went out to the Harder ranch—and where is he now?'

'But why would they bother with him?'

'They think,' chuckled Artemus, 'that he's a detective.'

'They think he's a detective?' snorted the sheriff. 'Of all the damn crazy ideas I ever heard. Why, the idea! He ain't, is he, Smoky?'

'Search me,' replied Artemus.

'He's a writer—ain't he?'

'That's what he says. He ain't wrote nothin'—yet.'

'Well, we can't do a thing until we know more,' decided the sheriff.

'I hope we know more,' sighed Artemus. 'I shore need that dude.'

Antelope Flats was thoroughly aroused over the report that Sally Harder and 'that damn dude,' as he was called, had disappeared. Jim Martin, the sheriff, had more posse-volunteers than he could handle. In fact, he didn't know where to start. There was no clue as to where they had gone. Flint Harder came in early, cursed everybody in a weak voice, and sat in his buckboard.

Mrs. Long and Mrs. Harder came to town to see Danny. They walked past the buckboard, but did not look at Flint Harder, who tried not to seem to notice them. Mañana Higgins, who had no fear

162

of Flint Harder's barking, went over and leaned against the buckboard.

'When is that damn-fool sheriff goin' to do somethin'?' asked Flint Harder.

'What?' asked Mañana wearily. 'We sat up all night tryin' to figure out what to do.'

'So did I,' replied Harder wearily. 'Where's that damn Hartley and his grinnin' pardner, anyway? Why don't they show up?'

Mañana shrugged his shoulders. 'They're gone, that's all I know.'

'Pulled out for good?'

'If they have, we're short two good rifles. Flint, yuh don't reckon Sally eloped with the dude, do yuh?'

Flint Harder almost strangled in his wrath.

'I didn't think they did,' said Mañana calmly. 'I heard folks talk about it.'

'Folks are sayin' *that?*' queried Harder huskily.

'Said they didn't blame her if she did—livin' with you thataway.'

Flint Harder actually flinched, and his hands clenched on his knees.

'I didn't think you was that bad,' said Mañana. 'I happen to know you sent Nell two hundred dollars in the mail.'

Flint Harder looked sharply at Mañana, a puzzled expression in his eyes.

'What did you say?' he asked.

'Aw, don't bluff about it, Flint. You sent Nell

two hundred dollars in the mail the other day. She don't know who sent it, but I reckon she has an idea. And she can sure use it, too. I thought at first it was Jim Martin, but he said he didn't.'

'Oh, yeah,' said Flint Harder absently. 'She didn't know.'

'Maybe she guessed. Well, I've got to be staggerin' along, Flint.'

For a long time Flint Harder sat there, staring at the rumps of the two horses. Artemus Day came along. His big hat fitted better with the lump on his head, and one side of his chin was purple.

Flint Harder looked at Artemus. 'Come over here,' he said.

Artemus stopped and looked at him. 'Yuh ain't shootin' topknots t'day, are yuh?' he asked.

'I want to talk to yuh.'

Artemus went over against the wheel of the buckboard.

'Can yuh write?' asked Harder.

'Can I write? Huh! Yo're dang right I can—a little. Why?'

'Would yuh do somethin' for me—and then forget it?'

'Anythin' I'd do for you—I'd want to forget, Flint.'

'All right, you little *mofeta*. Go over to the post office, get an envelope, and address it to Mrs. Dean Harder. Put a stamp on it and bring it to me. Here's two-bits.'

'Well, I'll be a dry-nurse to a dinny-sour! Oh, sure, I'll do it.'

'And forget it, Smoky?'

'I may not forget it, but I shore won't peddle it around.'

It was quite a task for Artemus to address the envelope. There were inkspots and erasures, but he got it all on the envelope, which he took back to Flint Harder.

'I'll remember this, Smoky,' said Flint Harder. 'Much obliged.'

Artemus was so shocked at being thanked by Flint Harder that he merely nodded and walked away. Down near the sheriff's office he met Mañana.

'How'r yuh comin', Artemus?' asked Mañana.

'All right. The swellin' is goin' down a little. Say, Mañana, what does *mofeta* mean?'

'In Mexican,' smiled Mañana, 'it's just plain skunk.'

Artemus turned and looked toward the buckboard, a block away.

'Yeah, and I'll remember that, too,' he muttered.

'What did yuh say?' queried Mañana.

'Just kinda talkin' to m'self,' replied Artemus.

Mrs. Long had been in the jail, talking with Danny. The sheriff left them alone in there, and was sitting at his desk when she came out.

'I'm so worried about Sally,' she said. Jim Martin nodded.

'I tried to get Nell to come here with me,' she said quietly.

Jim Martin turned his head and looked out the window.

'She don't feel that you want to see her,' continued Mrs. Long.

'I know,' he said slowly. 'Nell's proud. I reckon I was wrong, sayin' what I did when her and Dean got married. If she don't want to come, I guess she is justified. I don't deserve to see her.'

'Where are Mr. Hartley and Mr. Stevens?' she asked.

'They went away last night,' he replied. 'I don't know where they went. Everybody seems to want them.'

'Mr. Hartley makes you feel that everything is all right.'

'I wish he could make me feel that way.'

Mrs. Long left the office and met Artemus at the doorway.

'Howdy, Mrs. Long,' he grinned. 'How's Danny?'

'Just fine, Smoky.'

'He's better off than the rest of us, then.'

'How is your head this morning?'

'I'm jist scared to death that it's goin' to be all right—thank yuh.'

Jim Martin looked up as Artemus came in.

'I hope yuh find my boss,' Artemus said. 'I'd

166

hate to go back punchin' cows at forty a month—after what I've had.'

'What did he pay yuh?'

'Hundred a month and my board and room.'

'That's more than I make.'

'That's more than yo're worth, Jim. Danny Long's the first prisoner you've had in four years—and he had to be tattled on by a drunken Swede.'

'I reckon yo're right, Smoky; we haven't done much.'

'Aw, shucks, I didn't mean it that way. Yo're all right. I feel kinda mean today. Mebbe it's because I got banged around last night.'

'So they asked you if Montgomery is a detective, eh?'

'Yeah. Imagine that!'

'Smoky, just *what* do you know about him?'

'Aw, he's just what he says he is, Jim. He's read letters to me from his father, and the old man sure gives him hell—and sends money. His old man has got plenty money, too. Owns a couple banks and a few railroads. Maybe he did have an idea of bein' a detective, 'cause he sent his old man a telegram sayin' he believed he'd turn detective. The old man wired back, "You've got to do somethin' besides turn." '

'Smoky,' said the sheriff thoughtfully, 'can you write?'

'Can I—well, yeah, I can—some.'

'Good enough to write an address on a envelope?'

Artemus looked at him thoughtfully and a bit puzzled.

'I have done such a thing,' he said quietly.

The sheriff took an envelope from a desk drawer, shoved it over to Artemus, and gave him a pen.

'This,' he said quietly, 'is just between me and you, Smoky. Write on there, "Mrs. Dean Harder, Antelope Flats, Arizona."'

With his tongue in his cheek, Artemus hunched over the desk and laboriously scrawled the address—not good, but legible. Jim Martin looked at it closely, thanked Artemus, and put the envelope in his desk.

'Much obliged, Smoky,' he said. 'Don't ever mention it.'

'Yo're welcome,' said Artemus.

He went outside and walked up the street, still puzzled. Nick Higby and Pete Soboba were talking with Flint Harder at the buckboard.

Higby said: 'I don't care what the sheriff does; me and Pete are goin' to put on a search. We're takin' some grub and water along, because we might be gone for a while.'

'All right,' said Flint Harder wearily, 'and thank yuh, Nick.'

The two men went to get their horses. Artemus leaned against a porch-post and rubbed his jaw.

Higby and Soboba starting out on a personal hunt, and might be gone for a while. Where would they be going? wondered Artemus. Why start out without a definite destination? Or did they have one?

Artemus went back to the stable and saddled his horse.

CHAPTER XI

HASHKNIFE AND SLEEPY HAVE A POOR NIGHT'S REST

IT WAS just after dark when Hashknife and Sleepy left Antelope Flats and they rode all night, traveling east across the hills. There was a full moon, which made for good traveling. Early in the morning they stopped to rest the horses and eat a bite of food. They were a long way from Antelope Flats. There were no fences, no ranches in those hills, and they saw no cattle. There were plenty of deer.

Always they held to an easterly direction, not hurrying, avoiding hard climbs. At times Hashknife led the way to the north or south, cross-cutting the range, looking for a possible cattle-trail, but always they swung back to the east.

It was nearly sundown as they came out on a ridge, and saw a group of weatherbeaten ranch-houses in a clump of cottonwoods on the flat below them. An old wooden windmill creaked in the vagrant breeze, and a few head of cattle and horses loafed along the fences.

'That,' said Hashknife wearily, 'must be the Circle JR, belongin' to Jack Rett, whoever he is.

I hope they won't mind feedin' us and givin' us a bed for the night.'

'Mind?' grunted Sleepy. 'Let 'em try it. When I get this hungry, I'll eat—and I won't even ask permission. C'mon; there's smoke comin' from the stovepipe.'

They rode down past the old corrals and stopped near the kitchen doorway. Someone in the kitchen was singing in a cracked, off-key voice:

'Oh, bury me-e-e not on the lo-o-one pra-a-ree-e-e—'

'That all depends on how yuh can cook,' said Sleepy.

The man came to the door and shaded his eyes with his hand. He was grizzled and unkempt, wearing a faded shirt hanging out of his overalls, and an old pair of moccasins. Around his waist was a very dirty floursack apron.

'Who the hell are you?' he demanded as Hashknife came up to the doorway.

'I'm the man you didn't know,' replied Hashknife. 'How's chances for somethin' to eat?'

He looked searchingly at Hashknife and then at Sleepy.

'All right, I guess,' he said. 'Where yuh from?'

'Can't we leave that until after we eat?' asked Sleepy. 'It'll take a long time in the tellin'.'

'Drifters, eh? Well, you shore drifted into a hell of a country.'

'Don't yuh like it?' asked Sleepy.

'I ain't been here long enough to know.'

'A newcomer, eh?'

'Yeah—ten years.' The cook spat disgustedly. 'Damn place ain't fit to git drunk in. If yuh feel dudish, there's the wash-basin, and yuh can git water at the windmill. Mostly, we don't bother.'

'What spread is this?' asked Hashknife.

'Circle JR.'

'Boys are all out, eh?'

'Uh-huh. My name's Panamint, so called because I ain't never been in the Panamints. Born in Kansas, raised in Oklahomy, got chased to New Mexico, and came here of my own accord.'

'Can yuh cook?' asked Sleepy.

'That,' said Panamint, 'has been argued over for ten years. Put yore horses in the stable and give 'em some hay. Say! Yuh don't happen to know all the words of "Bury me not," do yuh?'

'No,' replied Hashknife.

'Now, ain't that hell? I ask everybody. All I've ever knowed is the first line, and I've shore sung her to shreds in ten years. Well, I'll rustle up a little grub for yuh.'

Hashknife and Sleepy did justice to a meal of

roast beef, baked beans, and boiled potatoes. Hashknife and Sleepy solved the question as to whether Panamint was a good cook or not. He wasn't. But hunger was appeased and their belts tightened. Panamint told them that the crew of the Circle JR consisted of five men, plus Jack Rett, who owned the spread.

Panamint was a little vague on the number of cattle, and whether Rett was making any money. He seemed a little suspicious and inclined to evade any direct questions. He did want to know who they were and what they were doing there, but they were as evasive as he.

The old ranch-house was of two stories, and Panamint showed them a room upstairs where they might sleep. It contained only a bed and some few blankets, but it was sufficient. There was one window, which Hashknife managed to open so they could have some fresh air.

'What do yuh think of the place?' asked Sleepy quietly, as they got ready for bed.

Hashknife shook his head. 'I'm leary of it, Sleepy. Panamint didn't want us here, but he couldn't get out of it. Better sleep with yore boots on, 'cause yuh never can tell.'

It was about midnight when Hashknife quietly awoke Sleepy.

'I think the boys are back,' he whispered.

They both got out of bed, and Hashknife opened the door a few inches. They could hear

174

footsteps and voices down in the main room, and a lamp had been lighted. Someone was yelling for Panamint. Their voices indicated that they had been drinking.

Panamint evidently joined them, because they were clamoring for something to eat. Panamint must have told them about the strangers in the house, because there was absolute silence for a few moments.

Then a man asked in a quiet voice, 'Didn't they tell yuh who they are, Panamint?'

Panamint's reply was inaudible.

Another voice said, 'A tall one and a shorter one, eh? Where'd they come from?'

'I dunno. Just a couple drifters, I reckon.'

'You reckon! Drifters don't come this way. Must be from Lost Horse Valley. Damn it, Panamint, you—'

'Wait a minute, Jack,' said another voice. 'Yuh don't suppose—' and the rest was inaudible.

The men seemed to move around uneasily.

Finally a voice said, 'If it is, what in hell are they doin' over here? If Les was here, he'd know.'

'Wait a minute,' said a voice with authority. 'If it's who we think it is, we'll take care of 'em. Listen here—' The voice was lowered.

'We'll have Panamint call 'em,' said another, after a dull buzz of conversation. 'When we get 'em down here—' and the voice faded.

Hashknife carefully closed the door and led the way over to the open window.

'Not wishin' to kill anybody,' he whispered, 'we'll move out.'

Even hanging at full length, it was quite a drop, but they landed safely and hurried down to the stable, where they saddled and took their horses outside. They could see a light in the window of the room they had vacated, and someone was leaning out of the window.

They rode a short distance away and drew up. They could hear footsteps pounding across the yard and down to the stable. The door banged open and in a few moments a man yelled, 'Their horses are gone!'

Someone up at the house was swearing at somebody else for talking too loudly.

Panamint said: 'So that was Hashknife Hartley, eh? Wish I'd have known it when they came.'

'You prob'ly saved us from havin' a funeral,' remarked another voice, and they went back into the house.

'Bad, bad boys,' remarked Hashknife. 'Well, anyway, we're not hungry.'

'What's to be done?' asked Sleepy.

'There's a hill over there,' replied Hashknife, pointing in the darkness. 'We'll hive up over there and see what they do in the mornin'.'

'Damn Bob Marsh!' groaned Sleepy.

'Amen,' added Hashknife.

• • •

There was little of the dude about Alexander Hamilton Montgomery. He was dirty of face, his hair matted, his gaudy clothes torn and soiled, and he had no glasses. There was a red welt running from above his left eyebrow nearly to the crown of his head, and it had bled enough to mat his hair. The left eye was slightly discolored. And in addition to all this, Alexander Hamilton Montgomery was securely bound, hand and foot, and lying on the hard floor of an old shack.

Near him, also bound, but sitting on an old blanket, was Sally Harder. Sally was uninjured, but her face was dirty, and she was not a bit happy. A grizzled old rawhider, dirty and unkempt, was mixing biscuits in the top of a flour-sack. He wore an old patched shirt, misfit overalls, which were held up by a piece of rope in lieu of suspenders, and an old pair of boots from which the heels had been knocked off. Belted around his expansive waist was a very serviceable-looking belt and a holstered Colt.

'Are you awake, Monty?' asked Sally wearily.

'Yes,' replied Monty weakly. 'What happened?'

The old man chuckled. 'I told yuh he'd wake up after while. I've knowed fellers to sleep the clock around after a belt over the head.'

'What happened?' repeated Alexander Hamilton Montgomery.

177

'Don't you remember the fight at the stable?' asked Sally.

'Yes, I—why, certainly—I remember.'

'That was last night.'

'Oh! Last night? What is it now?'

'It's past noon next day. How does your head feel?'

'It simply doesn't, Sally. But—where are we?'

'Are yuh good at guessin'?' asked the old cook.

'I suppose I am.'

'All right—guess.'

'Do you mean I have been asleep since last night?'

'Naw,' replied the old cook. 'You woke up seven-eight times, crazy as a loon. Me and the girl was worried about yuh.'

'But why are we tied up? We haven't done anything.'

The old man cackled and slapped his knee.

'Is that funny to you?' asked Sally.

'It shore is. Innercent as a lamb, ain't he?'

'Who are you?' asked Montgomery.

'Me? The boys call me Sody. And I'm boss here, and don'cha forget it. I'd as soon slit yore neck as look at yuh.'

'A very pleasant thought,' sighed Montgomery.

Sody poked some wood into the little sheet-iron stove, dusted his hands off on his overalls, and sat down on a box to fill his pipe.

'So yo're a detective, eh?' he sneered.

178

'Am I?' queried Montgomery.

'Yeah. And yore old man is rich.'

'What does that have to do with it?'

'We kill two birds with one stone. You get what's comin' to yuh, after we git a hunk of the old man's money. Good idea, eh?'

'Whose idea was that?' asked Sally.

'I can't tell yuh that, my dear.'

'But why keep me here? My father isn't rich—and I am not a detective.'

Sody took his pipe from his mouth, spat against the side of the stove, and shook his head.

'All I know is the boss said you was gettin' too damn smart. It's his business—not mine. All I'm supposed to do is to see that both of yuh are kept here safe. There won't nobody find yuh here; so yuh may as well behave. Just remember—I'm boss here.'

'Do you know Hashknife Hartley?' queried Montgomery.

Sody got to his feet and came over near the young man.

'What about Hashknife Hartley?' he asked.

'Nothing—I just wondered.'

'Yo're a liar. What about Hartley?'

'I just asked if you knew him.'

'Where did you know him?' asked Sody.

'At Antelope Flats.'

'At Antelope Flats? When?'

'I—I saw him yesterday.'

'Yo're lyin'. He ain't in this country.'

'Do you know Les Hart?' asked Sally.

'Of course I know him. What about Les Hart?'

'Hashknife Hartley killed him the other day.'

Sody turned, walked to the door, and opened it. After looking around, he closed the door and came back.

'Where's Hartley now—in Antelope Flats?' he asked.

'He and Sleepy Stevens left Antelope Flats yesterday,' said Montgomery. 'They borrowed rifles from the sheriff.'

'Where was they goin'?' demanded Sody anxiously.

'No one knows,' replied Montgomery. 'Hartley never tells what he is going to do.'

'So he killed Les Hart, eh? I think yo're lyin'.'

'I was along,' said Montgomery. 'Les Hart and two other men shot at us, but the other two got away when the sheriff came along.'

Sody swore under his breath, secured an old battered washpan, and quickly drew the fire from the little stove. He took the pan outside, doused the fire with water, and came back in.

'What was the idea of doing that?' asked Montgomery.

'Do you think I'm throwin' up smoke signals?' he snarled. 'From now on, we cook at night—if we cook at all.'

'Afraid of the officers, eh?' queried Sally.

'Officers! No officer will come here. But that damn bloodhound of a Hartley—yuh never can tell where he'll go.'

'Perhaps he has already seen your smoke,' suggested Montgomery.

'You two better hope he don't,' snarled Sody. 'You won't live to tell *him* anythin'.'

Sody went outside, fastened the door, and went away. They could hear cattle bawling near the shack.

'We're at somebody's ranch,' said Sally.

'My head hurts,' complained Montgomery. 'All of me except my head is numb. What do you suppose they'll do with us, Sally?'

'I don't know. You heard what he said about getting money from your father.'

'That might take months. Why, they don't even know where he is.'

'I don't know what will happen,' she sighed. 'Sody said that no one would ever find us here. It's a long way from Antelope Flats, unless they went in a circle. I was blindfolded and they led my horse. I know we climbed a lot of hills.'

'You seem very brave,' said Montgomery.

'I—I'm not—I'm frightened to death.'

'There's two of us,' said Montgomery miserably.

'I wonder what Artemus thinks.'

'What people think isn't going to do us any good.'

'I'm to blame for all of this,' said Montgomery. 'It was all because of the left-handed man, I'm sure.'

'Then your idea must have been right, Monty,' said Sally.

'That's right. Ed North must have been the left-handed man in the bank robbery.'

Sody opened the door and came in. He came over to them, an evil grin on his homely face.

'I thought you'd talk if I wasn't in here,' he said harshly. 'But I was there at the door, listenin'. Ed North, eh? You wanted to find a left-handed man. We wasn't sure you picked on Ed—but we know now. The boys will be glad to hear it.'

'So we were right, it seems,' said Monty.

'Just as right as I am when I tell yuh that yore guess won't never do you one damn bit of good, because you'll be too dead to cash in on it.'

'You don't dare kill him,' said Sally quickly.

Sody laughed shortly. 'You'll be with him, my dear. Our gang protects its boys—and yo're just as dangerous to us as he is.'

'I may be wrong,' said Montgomery, 'but I feel that a search is already being made for us.'

'Yeah?' sneered Sody. 'By who—that old sheriff? He couldn't find a black cow in a herd of sheep.'

'I was thinking about Hashknife Hartley and his partner,' said Monty.

Sody turned and glanced back at the door. It

was evident that he did not like the possibility of Hashknife and Sleepy being in that part of the country.

'They could find us,' said Sally quietly.

'Don't you believe it!' snapped Sody. 'Nobody can find us—except our own gang. I'm not scared of Hartley. If he comes, down here—'

'You admit that he might,' said Sally.

Sody growled a curse and went to get his bottle—but he didn't deny her statement.

Hashknife and Sleepy spent a rather uncomfortable night in the brush, and were awake early, watching the Circle JR ranch-house. They saw Old Panamint get wood for the stove and bring in water.

'I'd sure like breakfast,' yawned Sleepy. 'I crave food.'

'Tighten yore belt, pardner; we're a long way from food,' said Hashknife.

In about thirty minutes a man left the ranch-house and went down to the stable, where he saddled a horse. Two other men went down and talked with him for a while, after which he mounted and rode away, taking a westerly route, which brought him within about three hundred yards of where Hashknife and Sleepy sat on the brushy hill.

Hashknife smiled as the rider headed west, unhurried and alone.

'Do we foller him?' asked Sleepy.

'Later—maybe,' replied Hashknife. 'He looks like a decoy to me.'

The other men had gone back to the house.

After a half-hour of waiting, Hashknife said, 'Maybe I'm wrong, Sleepy. They might have— oh-oh!'

The two men left the house and went to the stable. Hashknife grinned, as they led out saddled horses, mounted quickly, and headed west. They did not follow the trail of the first man, but went angling out to the southwest, where a wide swale allowed them to swing west and keep out of sight.

Hashknife led the way back to their horses and they mounted quickly, after tightening their cinches, and started west again, taking advantage of the low places.

'That first man *was* a decoy, Sleepy,' said Hashknife, after a long ride down a slope and across a wide swale. 'They figured that we were still around and that we'd follow the first rider. He'll bear to the north, expectin' us to follow him and get lost. These last two whippoorwills are the ones we want to follow.'

'All right,' agreed Sleepy, 'but I'm dog-gone hungry. Where do yuh reckon them two are goin'?'

'Stealin' cows or to warn the rustlers that we're around. Either mission makes it easier for us.'

'You mean to say that the Circle JR are rustlers, Hashknife?'

'If they wasn't crooked, what about that talk last night? If we'd have stayed in that house last night we'd be first-class corpses this mornin'— and no questions asked. Yeah, I think they're connected with that rustlin' gang—but we've got to prove it.'

'And starve to death doin' it,' complained Sleepy.

'Yo're fat enough to live several days,' chuckled Hashknife.

'And then what—lay down and die?'

Hashknife laughed. 'Sleepy, when I went to school there was one sentence I had to write on the blackboard a hundred times. It was, "There is no diligence without great labor."'

'What,' asked Sleepy, 'is diligence?'

'I dunno, cowboy, but it must cover the huntin' for rustlers.'

'I'd use the word hunger in place of labor.'

For a long time they drifted along through the low places, guessing that the men they were following kept going in the same general direction. There was little brush on the hills and the trees were scattered.

After an hour or so they came out on a ridge and scanned the country. About a mile away, following down a swale, were the two men they had followed. They dropped back and went on. Hashknife chuckled.

'They're sure we followed the decoy, Sleepy,

185

or they'd be watching their back-tracks. Those two are plumb safe—in their own minds.'

'And with full bellies,' complained Sleepy. 'That's worth a lot. As far as we're *sure,* they could be perfectly innocent.'

'If you wait to be dead sure, pardner,' said Hashknife soberly, 'you'll either die young or never find out anythin'.'

'I hope I never die hungry,' said Sleepy soberly.

CHAPTER XII

'THE GENT I VENTILATED'

IN THE meantime, Artemus Day, 'knowed as Smoky,' was having a hard time. All day he trailed Nick Higby and Pete Soboba; trailed them far out of Lost Horse Valley, but lost them at nightfall. Artemus was disgusted with himself. He brought no food or water—and Artemus liked to eat. Here he was, miles from Antelope Flats, his horse weary.

Not that he was alarmed over having to spend the night out there, but he did crave food and drink. He picketed his horse with his lariat, used his saddle-blanket as a covering, and spent the night. Now that he had lost his quarry, all he had for his pains was a cold night and an empty stomach.

'But they was goin' some place,' he told himself. 'Them two *pelicanos* wasn't *lookin'*—they was goin'. And if I ain't mistaken, they wasn't far from that place. *Mañana*, I take me a look.'

Artemus shivered in the cold gray dawn as he saddled his horse.

'I wish I could eat grass,' he told the horse. 'Mebbe I'll get down to that before I get back to food.'

He rode a few miles farther, following the direction he believed taken by Nick Higby and Pete Soboba, and came to the rim of a deep canyon. Artemus thought it over and decided that this was El Diablo Canyon, of which he had heard but had never seen before.

'I'm shore a long ways from Antelope Flats,' he declared. 'Well, they didn't go into that canyon, so we better hunt for a way around it.'

It took Artemus a long time to find the head of the canyon, where he was no better off than before. As far as eye could see, there was only the brushy hills. A mile away was a tall hill, so Artemus decided to ride up there and see what he could see from that elevation.

It gave him a fair view of the country, but offered little. Far away he could see the blue haze of Lost Horse Valley, but there were a lot of broken hills before he could reach the Valley. But it was nice up there, sitting on a flat rock in the shade; so Artemus dozed, wondering just what he was going to do for something to eat, and also wondering what had become of Alexander Hamilton Montgomery and Sally Harder.

But after an hour or two of deep contemplation, he decided that life was little without nourishment. As he turned to go back to his horse, he saw a lone horseman. The rider was a quarter of a mile away on the crest of another hill, apparently looking over the country. Nick Higby rode a sorrel, Pete Soboba rode a black; so this was neither of them, because this man rode a gray.

'Prob'ly another hungry pilgrim,' decided Artemus. 'I'll cut his trail.'

It was not difficult for Artemus to locate the man. He was a big, unkempt denizen of the range, and he looked with evident disfavor upon Artemus. As a matter of fact, Artemus didn't like the man's looks one bit. Artemus did not wear a holstered gun, but shoved it inside the waistband of his overalls, and as he raised himself in the saddle the gun slid down. In the event of trouble, Artemus would almost have to undress himself in order to get that gun.

The man said, 'Just who the hell are you, anyway?'

'The name's Day,' replied Artemus.

'Day, huh? What'r yuh doin' up here?'

'Just—uh—lookin'.'

'Lookin', eh? What for?'

Artemus swallowed painfully and waved an arm in a vague gesture.

'Nice country,' he said.

'Yeah—nice country. But to hell with that; what's the idea of you bein' up here, all alone this-away?'

Artemus bristled. After all, who was this dirty-looking person to tell Artemus Day where he couldn't be? If that darn gun hadn't slipped—

'Where'd yuh come from?' demanded the man harshly.

'Antelope Flats.'

'Oh, yo're from Antelope Flats, eh? Wish yuh was back there?'

'Yeah, I kinda do,' admitted Artemus.

'It's a long walk,' said the man slowly, 'so yuh might as well start.'

'Walk? Why, you—'

A heavy Colt appeared in the man's hand and the muzzle of it was pointed straight at Artemus Day.

'Get off,' the man ordered.

Artemus got off slowly, and that gun slid down to his knee.

'Toss me that tie-rope.'

Reluctantly Artemus tossed him the end of the rope, which the man looped around his saddle-horn.

'I ort to drill yuh,' growled the man. 'Yeah, I ort to do that.'

Artemus held his breath. The man looked capable of doing just that.

'Na-a-aw, I don't want to play a joke on the buzzards,' he said.

'Much obliged,' muttered Artemus.

The man studied Artemus for a few moments, but to Artemus it seemed weeks. The little man shifted uneasily. He was afraid that the man on the horse might note the queer bulge above his boot-top.

'You bein' here—that's kinda funny,' remarked the man. 'No grub, no canteen. All alone, eh?'

'Do I look like I was with somebody?' retorted Artemus.

'Don't git smart, you little gopher. You came from Antelope Flats, eh?'

'I told yuh I did.'

'Yeah, that's right—but yuh didn't tell me why.'

'Nor I won't,' said Artemus stoutly. 'I ain't goin' to incriminate myself.'

The man laughed huskily. 'Yuh don't mean that the sheriff is after yuh.'

Artemus cuffed his hat back on his head.

'That's *my* business,' he said.

'Yeah, that's right. Well, I don't know what yuh done, and I don't care. But you better get out of this country. It ain't healthy for strangers. Go back and give yourself up. Let 'em hang yuh—who cares? And when I say for you to git out of here—I mean it—*sabe*?'

Slowly he relaxed and holstered his gun.

'I'll jist take yore horse and let yuh walk back to Antelope Flats. Next time I meet yuh, I'll shoot yore liver loose.'

Then he swung his horse around and rode away, leading Artemus's horse. Had he looked back he would have seen Artemus yank the left leg of his overalls from his boot-top, shake his leg violently, and grab a Colt forty-five before it hit the dirt.

The man was about a hundred feet away, both horses trotting, when Artemus leveled that big gun and squeezed the trigger. Artemus's horse swung out of line, as that heavy bullet went over its head, but the man didn't even turn his head. His body twisted a little and he seemed to lean a little more forward. Then they disappeared in the brush.

'Missed him!' groaned Artemus. 'Dog my cats, I missed him! My gosh, he never even looked back. Mebbe he's deef. Or did I miss him? He never even looked back! I jist wonder—'

Artemus went bowlegging his way down through the brush, gun in hand.

'I ain't goin' to walk until I have to!' he panted '. . . play a joke on the buzzards! I'll learn him.'

Recently Hashknife and Sleepy had had about the same luck as Artemus. Earlier they had been able to trail the two men, but in trying not to be seen themselves, they lost the track. It was a big country, with plenty of brush, and the ground was far too hard to leave hoofprints. After searching for an hour or more, Hashknife and Sleepy headed west, intending to go back to Antelope Flats, when they heard the rattling report of a shot.

They drew up and listened. The shot was not far away, but it was difficult to tell in just what direction, because of the multiple echoes.

'Mebbe somebody took a shot at a deer,' suggested Sleepy.

'Might be,' nodded Hashknife, 'but I figure that anybody in these hills might also take a shot at us if they had a good chance.'

They moved on a short distance, when Hashknife jerked his horse up short. Down through a brushy swale, only a short distance away, came a rider, leading a saddled horse. The rider was acting queerly. He seemed to be leaning forward, as though searching the ground ahead of him. The man and the two horses came into a clearing just as the rider collapsed, falling forward across the horse's shoulder, where he slid to the ground as the frightened horse swung away from him. Both horses stopped against the brush, looking at the fallen rider.

Hashknife and Sleepy moved forward quickly and had just reached the man when a disheveled figure crashed down through the brush. It was Artemus, swinging the big gun in his hand. He stopped short, his eyes wide in astonishment.

'I'll be a dry-nurse to a dinny-sour!' he yelped. 'You fellers!'

'Artemus Day!' exclaimed Hashknife. 'What on earth—'

'He—he stuck me up and took my horse—so I popped him!'

'And so you popped him,' said Hashknife. 'I'll be darned!'

None of them knew the man, who was very, very dead.

'He—he never even turned around!' marveled Artemus.

'He couldn't,' said Hashknife quietly. 'That bullet hit him so hard that he didn't realize what happened. I don't see how he stayed on that horse at all.'

'He had it comin',' declared Artemus. 'Stealin' my horse and makin' me walk back to Antelope Flats. Said he had a notion to shoot out my liver.'

'Lookin' at the gent,' remarked Sleepy, 'I believe yuh, Artemus.'

Hashknife looked up from his examination of the man.

'Recognize the gray horse, Sleepy?' he asked. 'That's the decoy.'

'That's right. Artemus, how come he didn't take yore gun?'

'He never seen it. The darn thing slipped down m' pant-leg, and I had to wait until he pulled out before I could shake it loose.'

Hashknife squatted on his heels and rolled a cigarette as he considered the dead man. Finally he said, 'Artemus, what are you doin' up here— alone?'

'My gosh, that's right—you don't know the news. There's been a lot of happenstances since you two left Antelope Flats. Listen—'

194

And Artemus told them the whole story about the left-handed cowboy, his experience in the hotel room, the missing Alexander Hamilton Montgomery and Sally Harder. He told them of how he followed Nick Higby and Pete Soboba all the way from Antelope Flats, only to lose them near El Diablo Canyon.

'I heard Nick Higby tell Flint Harder that him and Pete was goin' to search the country,' declared Artemus. 'Then I got my horse and trailed 'em, but they never searched a damn bit, Hashknife.'

'Why did yuh trail them, Artemus?' asked Hashknife.

'Well, I—I didn't have nothin' else to do—and I wanted to do somethin'. After all, I've lost my bank-roll. No dude, no salary.'

'He's a mercenary little devil,' remarked Sleepy. 'Artemus, yuh don't happen to have some ham and aigs in yore pocket, do yuh?'

'Why speak of love?' asked Artemus.

Hashknife ground the light off his cigarette, and proceeded to search the dead man's pockets. In a hip-pocket of his overalls was a flat package, wrapped in paper. Inside was nine hundred and sixty dollars in currency. There was also a slip of paper, on which was penciled:

$$96 \times 20 = 1920.$$
$$\text{One Half} = 960.$$

Hashknife studied the piece of paper closely, folded it up with the money, and put it in his pocket.

'I suppose yuh have to sell 'em cheap when yuh steal 'em,' he said.

'What was that?' asked Sleepy.

'Just talkin' out loud,' smiled Hashknife. 'Well, I reckon we've got to pack this *hombre* down to the sheriff.'

'I s'pose,' sighed Artemus.

They caught the two horses and roped the dead man to his own saddle.

'Cinch him on good,' grunted Sleepy, tugging on a rope. 'We're goin' fast, 'cause I'm hungry, and it's a long ways to ham and aigs.'

They rode out of the swale, with Hashknife in the lead, and with Artemus, leading the extra horse, bringing up the rear. They were just going over the top of the swale when a bullet smashed into the fork of Artemus's saddle and the report of the rifle rattled across the hills. Another sighed past Sleepy's head and he ducked low. Artemus let loose of the lead-rope, which uncoiled from the saddle-horn as he spurred ahead.

'I ain't botherin' with no dead men!' yelped Artemus, and went galloping down the other side, his horse buck-jumping the brush.

More rifle bullets seeped through the brush, but all three riders were over the top of the swale. Hashknife and Sleepy dismounted quickly,

196

yanked their rifles from their saddles, and crouched in the brush. Artemus crossed the swale and was on the opposite rim, when his big, expensive Stetson hat went sailing. Artemus lost no time in dismounting.

Hashknife and Sleepy could hear Artemus swearing over his mutilated hat. They could not see anyone, but they knew that no one would dare come over that rim. The brush was too heavy for anyone to move without being heard.

'Can yuh see anybody, Artemus?' called Sleepy, and a faint voice replied, 'I'm down so damn flat I couldn't even see my own face in a mirror.'

There was a period of silence, and then Artemus began yelling; 'There they go! There they go! The sons-of-guns stole m' dead man!' And Artemus emptied his sixshooter in their direction, swearing after every shot.

'Run, you grave-robbers!' he shrilled.

Hashknife and Sleepy stood up and walked back to their horses, while Artemus continued his vituperations. They rode up to him and he caught his horse.

'Which way did they go?' asked Sleepy.

'Straight east—and goin' like hell,' replied Artemus. 'They must have sneaked in and caught that four-legged hearse, 'cause they was way out there when I saw 'em. Look at that hat, will yuh? Top busted right out of it!'

'Good thing it didn't fit,' said Sleepy dryly.

'Yeah, that's right. I'd look funny with my head fuzzed up thataway.'

'Did you see what color horses they was ridin'?' asked Hashknife.

'A sorrel and a pinto.'

'All three from the Circle JR,' said Hashknife. 'I'll bet they were to meet that decoy person right here and see what he knew.'

'And he ain't talkin',' added Artemus. 'He-ey! You say they're from the Circle JR?'

'That's right,' nodded Hashknife.

'Whee-e-e, brother!' snorted Artemus. 'I thought I'd seen that mug before. The gent I ventilated was Jack Rett, the owner of the Circle JR.'

'Are yuh sure?' asked Hashknife.

'Yo're darn right! I never seen him but once in my life, but yuh can't mistake a face like that. Brother, when I shoot—I take the top man.'

'No conscience whatever,' sighed Sleepy.

'Do yuh expect me to break down and cry?' asked Artemus. 'That sidewinder took m' horse away from me and threatened to shoot me.'

'Well, anyway,' said Sleepy, 'they took the job off our hands. We might have a hard job explainin' things to the sheriff. This way, it's their problem, not ours. If there's any argument, we'll swear that you killed him. What yuh should have done was to take his scalp.'

'He darn near took mine,' said Artemus.

Hashknife rolled and lighted another cigarette,

198

his eyes thoughtful. 'You spoke about El Diablo Canyon, Artemus,' he said quietly.

'Uh-huh. It's over thataway—two-three miles, I think.'

'Big canyon?'

'Plenty. Must be seven-eight miles long, and if yuh fell into it yore whiskers would grow three inches before yuh hit bottom.'

'I'd like to see it.'

Sleepy groaned. 'Anythin' to keep me away from the feed-bag.'

'As fer me,' remarked Artemus, 'I hate tripe. I'd jist as soon eat the strings off my saddle. But if I had a plate of tripe right now—'

'I'd take it away from yuh at the point of a gun,' said Sleepy, 'and I hate it worse than you do.'

'We'll take a look at El Diablo Canyon,' said Hashknife.

CHAPTER XIII

IN EL DIABLO CANYON

THINGS were not so pleasant for Sheriff Jim Martin. Harassed by Flint Harder, the prosecuting attorney, and 'most everybody in Antelope Flats, he sat in his office, mad enough to resign. There had been no move made by the kidnapers, no communication of any kind; and there was nothing to indicate where Sally Harder and Alexander Hamilton Montgomery might be. What was the use, he argued, of a sheriff running around on a fruitless search?

Flint Harder wanted his daughter back, and he wanted her right now. Most of his time was spent on the seat of his buckboard out in front of the hotel, waiting for news. Few went to him, because of his bitter tongue. Nick Higby and Pete Soboba had not returned, and he heard that Artemus 'Smoky' Day was also missing. It seemed to him that everybody in Lost Horse Valley was keeping an eye out for a clue, except Jim Martin, the sheriff.

Henry Clews, the elderly postmaster, left the post office and went down to the sheriff's office, hurrying. That was news, because Clews was never known to be in a hurry. He went into the office and leaned across the sheriff's desk.

'Jim,' he said, 'I've got something!'

From his pocket he removed a soiled envelope and placed it on the sheriff's desk. Printed on it in scrawling capitals, written with a soft lead-pencil, was the address:

JAMES A. MONTGOMERY,
WALL STREET,
NEW YORK CITY

'What about it?' asked the sheriff curiously.

'This,' replied Clews. 'That's the name of the dude's father. I've seen it on his envelopes 'most ever' day.'

Jim Martin leaned back and considered the envelope closely. It was soiled and wrinkled, with some of the letters smudged. It might have been carried in a chaps-pocket for some distance.

'Under the circumstances, I reckon I'll take a chance and open it,' he said slowly. 'It might tell us somethin'.'

Clews nodded. 'I hope it does, Jim.'

The envelope contained a single sheet of soiled paper, on which had been penciled:

We've got your son. If his life is worth $20,000 to you, send it to Jim Martin, the sheriff, Antelope Flats, Arizona. If he ain't worth it, don't do anything. We don't

202

mind killing him. We'll tell the sheriff
how to give us the money.

Yrs truly
The Lost Horse Gang

Jim Martin read it aloud, while Clews nodded
violently.

'I'm glad I spotted it,' he said. 'Now we know
he's been kidnaped.'

'And,' added the sheriff, 'if they don't collect
twenty thousand dollars from the dude's father—
they'll kill him. But this don't tell us where Sally
Harder is, Clews.'

The sheriff copied the letter, sealed it, and gave
it back to the postmaster.

'You better get that out on the first mail,' he
said. 'I'll send him a telegram right away.'

Mrs. Long came to see Danny, and the sheriff
went back to the cell with her, where he told them
both about the ransom letter.

'It didn't mention Sally Harder?' asked Mrs.
Long.

'Not a word. Anyway, they wasn't askin' the
dude's father for money for Sally Harder.'

'No, that is true,' admitted Mrs. Long.

'How is Nell?' asked the sheriff quietly.

'I'm glad you asked about her,' said Mrs. Long.
'Maybe you can unravel this mystery. Nell has
received three letters, all addressed by the same
person. In the first one was two hundred dollars,

in the second one was five hundred dollars, and in the last one, one hundred dollars. Eight hundred dollars, and not a scratch to show who sent them.'

Jim Martin grunted in amazement. Eight hundred dollars! All sent by the same person. He had sent her a hundred dollars, but he had no idea who had sent the other two amounts. If he could get his hands on Artemus Day—but Artemus was among the missing.

'Are you sure about the writing on the envelopes?' he asked.

'They are identical, Mr. Martin.'

Jim Martin shook his head. 'It's sure queer,' he said quietly.

Mañana Higgins met the sheriff in the office, and asked him about the ransom letter.

'Who told you, Mañana?' asked the sheriff.

'Flint Harder. Henry Clews told him, and Flint is rearin' straight up in his buckboard, cussin' everybody. Mebbe he thinks he'll get one for Sally. Mebbe he will, at that. Now what's to be done, Jim?'

'I'm wirin' to the dude's father. If he don't hurry, them dirty coyotes might kill the kid. The Lost Horse Gang! Can yuh imagine that?'

'I'm beginnin' to,' replied Mañana dryly. 'I wish I knew where Hashknife, Sleepy, and that damn Smoky Day are. They ain't stayin' away for fun. Sa-ay! I just wonder.'

'Wonder what?' asked the sheriff curiously.

'Hashknife was askin' a lot of questions about the Circle JR outfit. Wanted to know about Jack Rett, and what kind of a place he had. He looked through the brand register, and I seen him foolin' with a pencil, drawin' brands. Jim, do you reckon they went over to the Circle JR?'

'I don't know. I hope they come back and return my rifles.'

'You know Jack Rett, don't yuh, Jim?'

'Yeah, I know him—the homely devil. I wouldn't trust him from here to you.'

'That's it, Jim. Could Hartley be figurin' that mebbe Rett and his outfit—'

'They ain't even in Lost Horse Valley.'

'Oh, yuh mean the name of their gang. That don't mean nothin'. I knew a man who was born and raised in Cripple Creek and never got ten miles away in his life—and they called him Broadway. Names don't mean anythin'. 'Member New York Jones? Never was out of Colorado in his life.'

'Mañana,' said Jim Martin soberly, 'you seem to have hatched an idea. It'll give us a reason for leavin' Antelope Flats. I'm sick of seein' that scorpion of a Harder settin' there in his buckboard.'

'Yuh mean—headin' east, Jim?'

'Uh-huh. Rustle us enough grub for a couple days. Have Alphabet Anderson look after the

prisoner. Don't tell anybody where we're goin'—
and they might think we've got a clue.'

'Ain't we, Jim?'

'We ain't—all we've got is a destination.'

The plight of Sally and Alexander Hamilton
Montgomery had not improved with time. It
was bad enough to be bound hand and foot for
many hours, but Sody refused to build a fire and
do any cooking during the day, for fear of someone seeing the smoke. Once during the night,
Sody went out and talked with some men, far
enough away to prevent Sally and Montgomery
from hearing what was said. Sody had a bottle
of liquor when he came in, and seemed in better
spirits.

'What are they waiting for?' groaned Montgomery. 'If they are going to kill me, why wait?'

'Are yuh in a hurry to die?' asked Sody. 'If yuh
are, I've got a real sharp knife. It won't hurt yuh
much.'

Montgomery subsided. Sally was very brave,
but very weary. It seemed weeks since they came
to that shack. They hated even to ask Sody for
a drink of water, because he swore at them and
slopped the water all over their faces.

It was late in the afternoon when Sody heard
the sound of hoofs on the ground. He took his
gun in hand and went quietly outside.

'Someone coming,' said Sally. 'Listen, Monty.'

Sody said: 'Jack Rett—dead? My Gawd, what happened to him?'

They were unable to hear the reply, but one man said, 'Damn 'em, we had 'em dead to rights at the ranch, but somebody talked too loud, and they got away.'

After some low-toned conversation, which they could not hear, one of the men said: 'No, he didn't. Jack went out ahead, tryin' to draw 'em away, in case they were watchin' the ranch. They followed him.'

'But who's the third man?' asked Sody. 'Yuh say there was three?'

'That's right. They were takin' Jack away with 'em, but we made one of 'em drop the lead-rope. I don't know how we missed killin' some of 'em.'

'Are yuh sure it was Hartley?' asked Sody.

'Mighty sure.'

'And they're around here yet, eh?'

'We don't know—but we're not takin' any chances.'

'The hell you ain't!' snorted Sody. 'Comin' down here thataway. That Hartley could trail a snake across a lake. Chances!'

'Gettin' spooky, eh, Sody?'

'You bet I'm gettin' spooky! Me here alone with them two. Suppose I'm bushed, with them both here in my care? Who swings for it? Me! Don't tell me anythin' different. If I had my way, I'd kill 'em both—and be done with it.'

There was a period of low conversation, and Sody said; 'That letter has been posted. I think it's a loco idea. Suppose it does reach the man. It'll be weeks before it can be worked out. By that time everybody in Lost Horse Valley will be searchin'. And if Hartley suspects yore outfit, all hell can't save us. Damn it, they've already got Les Hart and Jack Rett. Don't tell me anythin' about it—I know plenty.'

The conversation quieted.

Sally whispered; 'Monty, it's the Circle JR outfit. Jack Rett was the owner. Les Hart was one of their gang. Monty, don't you hear me?'

In the gloom of the shack she could see Monty's right shoulder twisting, and he seemed to be breathing heavily. Then he sagged back.

'Sally,' he whispered huskily. 'Listen, Sally.'

'What is wrong?' she asked.

'I've got my right arm free!' he whispered.

'Sh-h-h-h!' she hissed. Horses were moving away, and in a few moments Sody came back and closed the door.

He picked up his bottle and took a big drink.

'Everythin' is all right,' he told them. 'In a few days the dude's father will be sendin' the money, and we'll let yuh go.'

'Both of us?' asked Sally.

Sody chuckled. 'I ain't so sure of you, my dear.'

'You don't know where my father lives,' said Montgomery.

'No? Well, smart-feller, we happened to get one of the envelopes yuh throwed away, which gives yore father's address. The letter has gone to him; so yuh might as well take it easy. We'll get the money.'

Sody drank again with satisfaction and stretched out on his bunk, but he was constantly alert. Any slight sound would send him to the doorway, where he would listen intently. It was nearly dark in the shack when Montgomery asked Sody for a drink.

Sody growled a curse, but got up and filled a cup.

'If you will please help me to sit up, we will not spill so much,' said Montgomery. 'It is difficult to drink in a reclining position.'

'Yuh talk like a dictionary, dude,' growled Sody. 'All right, I'll set yuh up.'

He leaned over Montgomery, clutched him by the shoulders, and began lifting. As Montgomery came to a sitting position, he twisted a little and his right fist, in a short, jolting uppercut, caught Sody just too high for a knockout. However, it knocked him down on the floor, where he sprawled, clawing around, trying to get up again. Montgomery's feet were bound, and his left hand, only partly loose, was of no use to him, but he twisted and rolled into Sody, trying to hit him again with his right fist.

But Sody was an old campaigner in rough-

and-tumble fighting. He was still dazed, but full of fight. He hit Montgomery on the side of the head, and tried to follow it up with a left-hand punch, but missed and fell across Montgomery. By that time Montgomery had his left hand loose, but it was so cramped that it was of little value. However, he wrapped his left arm around Sody's neck, and punched him several times with short right jabs. They were fighting silently in the half-light, like a couple of animals. Sody's left eye was fast swelling shut and Montgomery was bleeding from the nose.

Suddenly Sody tore himself loose, leaving part of his shirt in Montgomery's hand. He staggered to his feet, snarling like a wolf, as he fairly tore his gun from his holster. He was almost standing on Sally as he drew the gun, but before he could level it, Sally drew back her two bound feet and kicked ahead with all the strength in her body.

Her hard heels caught Sody's left kneecap, knocking him off balance, and the gun went off, pointed ceilingward. She kicked again, and Sody came down, hitting the side of his head against the rough wall. This time he didn't get up.

'My goodness!' exclaimed Montgomery. 'You did it, Sally!'

'Never mind that,' panted Sally. 'Get a knife and cut us loose.'

'Yes, of course. Stupid of me, I'm sure.'

Montgomery crawled over to the table, where he secured the butcher-knife, sawed the ropes off his ankles, and then released Sally, who cried out from the pain of returning circulation.

Montgomery mopped the blood off his face, picked up Sody's gun, and looked around, wondering what to do next.

'Find rope . . . tie Sody . . .' panted Sally painfully.

There were plenty of ropes in the shack, but Montgomery knew little about knots. However, he was willing, and in a few minutes Sody was trussed from end to end, blinking up at them. Sally lighted a lantern and they looked at Sody, who glared at them with his one good eye.

'Done in by a damn dude!' he wailed. 'I knowed I should have killed yuh both when I had the chance.'

'My goodness, he is still mean,' marveled Montgomery.

Sody gritted his teeth for a moment. 'Pizen as a rattler,' he admitted, 'and you'll find it out. You can't get away. In the first place, yuh can't *find* the way out, and if yuh did—you'd be shot.'

'At least,' retorted Sally, 'we're loose.'

Sody cackled loudly. 'Go ahead, sister; don't mind Old Sody. Try and get away.'

'We'll take the lantern,' said Montgomery.

'That's right. It'll make yuh an easy target.'

'Just where is this shack?' asked Sally.

'In the deepest part of El Diablo Canyon, sister.'

'But—they say—' faltered Sally.

'That there ain't no way in,' chuckled Sody. 'Well, there is, sister; wide enough to drive cows—if yuh can find it. Go ahead. I'll give yuh plenty time.'

'What is El Diablo Canyon?' asked Montgomery.

'Show him, sister. Show him El Diablo Canyon, where no man can go. They won't even find yore bones in here, dude. Better take it easy, travelin' in the dark. There's bottomless pot-holes—remember.'

They went outside. The little shack was hemmed in with brush and piles of huge boulders, probably invisible, except from straight overhead. Overhead was a strip of starlit sky, but all else was black. Somewhere a cow bawled softly.

Sally said, 'They must have cattle down in here, Monty.'

'Why not?' queried Montgomery.

'Of course, you wouldn't understand,' she said.

'All I care to understand is that I want to get you out of here and back home safely, Sally,' he said. 'I'm not much good in a place like this. Not much good any place, as far as that goes. But no matter what happens to us, I want you to know that I think you are the most wonderful girl I have ever met.'

'Thank you, Monty.'

'You saved my life when you kicked him on the knee. In another moment he would have fired. You are wonderful, Sally.'

'As a life-saver?' she asked.

'As a woman, Sally. If we ever get out of this place alive—'

'Let's do that first,' she suggested. 'The rest can wait.'

'You have very sensible ideas. By the way, I still have Sody's gun.'

'Be careful of it, Monty. You take the lantern and lead the way. Maybe we can find our way out of here.'

'Every step a prayer,' he said jauntily. 'Can you pray, Sally?'

'I am afraid not, Monty.'

'Neither can I, but if we ever get out of here alive, I'll learn.'

CHAPTER XIV

BEANS

HASHKNIFE sat on the rim of the canyon, while Sleepy and Artemus sprawled on their backs, comparing things they liked to eat. The sides of El Diablo were very brushy, in spite of their sheer cliffs, and it was difficult to get any view of the bottom. From down in the canyon came the sound of a muffled shot. At least, it sounded like a shot.

A buzzard came flapping its way up along the cliffs, turning and twisting as it gained altitude. Hashknife considered the buzzard, and nodded with satisfaction.

'That was a shot,' he told them. 'It scared that buzzard. There wasn't much echo, so the shot must have been fired inside a cave, inside a house, or with the muzzle close to an object.'

'I sure hope it wasn't against Alexander Hamilton Montgomery,' said Artemus soberly. 'I'd hate to go back to forty a month again.'

'And yore board and room,' added Sleepy.

'Board!' snorted Artemus. 'I'm weaned.'

'And it's forty miles to ham and eggs,' sighed Sleepy.

'Artemus,' said Hashknife, 'did you say that there's no way into El Diablo?'

'Never has been, as far as I know.'

'No outlet at the other end?'

'Nope. Both ends just alike, allee same angle-worm.'

'There's somebody down in there. That shot came from there.'

'Yeah, it sure sounded thataway. But you'll find that somebody learned a buzzard how to shoot. It's a funny world. Yuh didn't know that I was a professional envelope-director, did yuh?'

'I suppose there's a funny answer,' sighed Sleepy.

'There ain't. Yuh see—'

'Wait a minute!' snorted Hashknife. He got quickly to his feet, peering into the canyon.

'What did yuh see?' asked Sleepy anxiously.

'I saw a cow.'

'In that canyon?' jeered Artemus. 'Man, it must be hunger—not cows.'

'Mebbe a shadow,' suggested Sleepy. 'Man, it's almost sundown. If we are goin' to get back to Antelope Flats before—'

Hashknife hitched up his belt and looked around. 'You fellows can go back to Antelope Flats if yuh want to, but I'm goin' to find a way into that canyon.'

'Right over there is a slippery rock, pointin' down,' said Artemus. 'If yuh must do it—there's the place.'

'Make up yore minds,' said Hashknife quietly.

216

'There's food in Antelope Flats—none here.'

'If you can stand it, pardner—I can,' said Sleepy.

'And I can forget mine,' said Artemus, but added, 'I hope.'

They rode for about a mile, but it was getting too dark. Sleepy suggested that they stay there all night and make their search in daylight.

'I'm playin' a hunch,' said Hashknife. 'You boys stay here while I do some scoutin'. If I want yuh, I'll whistle like a mocker. You know the notes, Sleepy.'

Then he was gone. Even in high-heel boots Hashknife was as stealthy as a marauding Apache. It required a lot of time for him to cover a hundred yards. He stopped often and listened, feeling with each foot, avoiding broken twigs, his hands gently fending the brush, so it would not scrape across his clothes. Some sixth sense told him that he was, in the parlance of the old parlor game, getting warm. He crouched near the bole of an old gnarled tree, every sense alive.

Just ahead, through a thicket of mesquite, he saw a match lighted. He and Sleepy and Artemus were not the only ones on the rim of El Diablo Canyon that night. Slowly he made his way to the thicket, where he crouched again. Fifty feet ahead of him were two men, conversing in low tones.

Hashknife slid forward on the hard, rocky

ground, and began snaking his way through the mesquite. It was slow work. Each branch of mesquite is barbed, and they grow low. He had to unhook every barb before going ahead. But he had patience. Each slither brought him closer to the two men, and in a matter of fifteen minutes he was not over a dozen feet away, unseen and unheard.

One of the men was on his feet, apparently looking into the canyon, because he said: 'Damn that Sody! He must be drunk—runnin' around with a lighted lantern. Somebody's goin' to see that and—you stay here—I'm goin' down there and cuff the ears off that old fool.'

Hashknife could not see the horses, but he heard the creak of leather as the man mounted, and he saw the blur of horse and rider as they seemed actually to fall off into the canyon. He heard the slither of gravel from a trail as the hoofs slid.

The remaining guard at the top of the trail began humming a tune. Hashknife began snaking his way ahead. He was afraid that the man would hear the rasp of his clothes against the rocky ground, but the man kept on humming. At a distance of about ten feet Hashknife was low enough to see the silhouette of the man's head and shoulders against the sky. Evidently he was sitting on a rock.

Hashknife inched ahead, lifting on his elbows, almost breathless now. Then the man got to his feet, apparently looking down into the canyon. Then he said aloud, 'Where the hell's he goin' with that lantern?'

He turned quickly, as though starting over to his horse, when Hashknife grasped his ankles, throwing him flat on the ground. The startled yell from the man's throat was broken by his heavy fall, and the next moment Hashknife was sitting on him. But the man was powerful, and in spite of the weight on his back, got to his hands and knees, wheezing a curse. Then Hashknife's heavy forty-five banged against the side of his head, and he collapsed with a smothered grunt.

'One baby down, one see-gar,' panted Hashknife. He got to his feet and found the man's horse, where he took down the rope and came back.

One of the man's sleeves made an effective gag, and with forty feet of hard-twist rope, he was securely bound in a few moments.

Hashknife took the man's gun and went over to the top of the trail, where he sat down, lighted a cigarette, and waited for the other man, who came in about fifteen minutes, his horse heaving from the climb. He swung off and dropped his reins.

'That wasn't Sody!' he blurted. 'Sody's in the shack, nursin' a sore head—and them two have gone. They took the lantern, and Gawd only knows where they are now. The dude got a hand

219

loose and whipped Sody, and then they tied him up. Hell's to pay, and no pitch hot!'

Whap! Hashknife's chop with that gun-barrel was no love-tap. He caught the man in his arms and dragged him over beside his companion, where he used the man's own rope to hog-tie him securely.

Then he stepped away, cupped his hands, and whistled the call of the mocking-bird, but louder than any mocker ever called. After a few moments the call came back to him. Sleepy and Artemus were on their way, hurrying through the brush and over the rocks. Hashknife called again, but quietly this time, and the answer came back immediately.

In a few moments they forced their way through the mesquite, and Hashknife said, 'Step easy over there; I've got us a couple pets.'

'Who are they?' asked Sleepy.

'I never peeked yet. Didn't want to light too many matches. Here's the layout,' he explained, and told them what had happened.

'You mean—there's a trail into El Diablo?' asked Artemus.

'Go over and look at them two horses,' said Hashknife.

'What for?'

'See if they've got wings.'

'I'll be a dry-nurse to a dinny-sour!' gasped Artemus.

'What's next?' asked Sleepy.

'Alexander Hamilton Montgomery and Sally Harder are down there,' replied Hashknife. 'No doubt this feller turned Sody loose and gave him a gun—whoever Sody is—and he's on their trail. We've got to beat Sody to it.'

'A shack down there, Artemus,' said Sleepy. 'Does that mean anythin'?'

'Nutriment!' grunted Artemus. 'Food! What are we waitin' for?'

'I could eat a snack,' admitted Hashknife, 'but we've got work ahead of us tonight. C'mon, and go easy. We don't know this trail, and we don't know what's at the end of it. I'll go ahead, and yuh better dig in yore heels, because it must be steep. And hang to the inside, gents; it's a long way to the bottom. C'mon.'

The trail was rather narrow, twisting along the side of the canyon wall, and it seemed well screened with brush. It was dark down there, too; so dark that they brushed in close to the inside wall, feeling ahead for each step, as they went deeper and deeper into the depths of El Diablo.

They finally reached the bottom, still in thick brush, but they were able to find the opening which led to the shack. There was no light in the place. They felt along the rough wall until they discovered the door which was not fastened.

'Go easy,' whispered Hashknife. 'There's still the man they called Sody to contend with; and any of this gang are as dangerous as rattlers.'

There was no one in the shack. They lighted a candle and looked the place over carefully.

'Beans!' grunted Artemus, grabbing a can and tossing one to Sleepy.

Hashknife picked up an end-gate rod from a wagon, which had been bent into a branding-iron. It was a small U; too small to constitute a brand by itself.

Sleepy and Artemus were cutting the tops out of cans with their pocketknives when a voice said from the doorway, 'Don't move, or I'll drill all of yuh!'

It was Sody. There was blood on the side of his face and his left eye was nearly swollen shut, but he was as mean as a wolf. His good eye took in the situation, but he seemed at a loss what to do next. The candle flickered in a draft from the doorway, causing their shadows to dance on the wall.

'Trapped yuh, eh?' he gritted.

Hashknife smiled. 'You're the one who is trapped,' he said quietly.

'Me?' Sody leaned forward, his knuckles white, as he gripped the gun in his right hand. 'How'm I trapped?'

'Behind yuh!' exclaimed Sleepy. Sody's nerves were not in good shape, because he fell for the oldest trick on earth and before he could turn back Sleepy's can of beans hit him square in the head. It knocked him off balance, and before he could recover, Hashknife knocked him all the way down, and took his gun.

Sleepy recovered the can of beans and continued to open it. Artemus sat down on a corner of Sody's bunk and ate beans off his knife-blade.

Sody recovered quickly and glared one-eyed at them.

'Where's the dude and the girl?' asked Hashknife.

'What are yuh talkin' about?' asked Sody. 'Ain't nobody in the canyon but me. I'm a trapper.'

'Yeah, I know,' said Hashknife quietly. 'Predatory hunter, eh?'

'Yeah, yeah, that's it!'

'You let two of 'em get away awhile ago, but I got 'em at the top of the trail. They're all tied up for shipment.'

Sody blinked his good eye. 'Yuh mean—what do yuh mean?'

'How long have you been stayin' down here?'

'Oh, a long time. I built this cabin.'

'Yeah—who for?'

'For me. Like I told yuh, I'm a trapper and—'

'I know. But you didn't trap us. Now, I'd like to have yuh tell me where that young fellow and the girl went. There's the ropes they had on—and the knife they used to cut 'em loose.'

'Them old ropes? Shucks, them ropes have been there—'

'Since they cut 'em off. Remember, I was at the top of the trail. One of yore bunkies saw the lantern and came down here to see what you was doin'. I knocked out the other one and tied him up. When this other *pelicano* came back, I let him tell me all about it in the dark, before I packed him with his pardner. So don't try to tell me about you bein' a trapper. Yore name's Sody, ain't it?'

'Gawd!' breathed Sody.

'Which way did they go, Sody?'

'I—I don't know. Hell, I couldn't find 'em— and I know the canyon. Mebbe they fell into a pot-hole. There's a lot of 'em, deep as hell, where the water used to go out. They'll never get out if they ever fell into one.'

Somewhere a cow bawled softly. Hashknife looked intently at Sody.

'You don't happen to trap cows down here, do yuh, Sody?' he asked.

'No, I—' Sody hesitated and looked the other way.

Hashknife picked up the wagon-rod and looked at Sody.

'For instance,' he said, 'yuh can take a little iron like this and make a JR out of a Quarter-Circle H. It won't be perfect, but it'll pass. And yuh can also put that little U iron on the end of an R, and make it JR. And then yuh can complete the circle from a quarter-circle, or from a rocker on the Rockin' R brand.'

Sody took a deep breath and looked one-eyed at Hashknife. 'Is yore name Hashknife Hartley?' he asked huskily.

Hashknife nodded. 'Yeah, that's my name.'

'Gawd!'

'Wasn't expectin' me, was yuh, Sody?'

'They—I—we knowed you was around. Damn 'em, I told 'em—aw, what's the use? You got Slim Sherrod and Tex McCall—and Jack Rett is dead.'

'Who else is in the gang, Sody?'

Sody glared at Hashknife. 'You've found out so damn much—find out the rest. I'm keepin' my mouth shut.'

'And one eye,' added Sleepy, throwing the can aside.

'Tie him up,' said Hashknife. 'We're wastin' time here.'

While Sleepy and Artemus trussed Sody tightly, Hashknife examined the shack for any more evidence. Under the bunk was a fifty-pound box of high-percentage dynamite, together with some fuse and caps. There was extra bedding and plenty of canned goods, some extra cartridges, and at least a hundred feet of half-inch hard-twist rope, to be cut in lariat lengths. The shack was fairly well equipped.

'Want us to gag him?' asked Artemus. 'I've got a awful dirty rag.'

'Might as well,' smiled Hashknife. 'No use makin' him listen to his own cussin'.'

'I'll git you if it's the last thing I ever do, you little bowlegged scorpion,' wailed Sody. 'I'll cut yore heart out and . . . ugg-glugg-mm. . . .'

'Artemus, you'll never know what he'd do with yore heart,' chuckled Sleepy, as he tied the gag tightly. They left the candle burning and went outside.

CHAPTER XV

DYNAMITE

SALLY and Montgomery fought their way through brush and over rocks, guided by the lantern-light, until they were both exhausted. There were cattle all through the brush, staring dumbly at the light and then crashing away through the brush. Then Montgomery stepped into a hole, fell full length, and flung the lantern against a rock. That was the end of the illumination.

'Now we are in a fix!' groaned Montgomery. 'We can't even move without a light.'

'Even if we can't go any place, they can't find us,' said Sally cheerfully.

'When it gets daylight they'll find us, Sally.'

'At least we're not tied hand and foot, Monty.'

They snuggled in close together against a rock. There was a cold draft down that canyon, and they were not too warmly clad.

'I have still got that gun,' he told her. 'I couldn't hit the side of a barn with it. At least, that is what Artemus says of my marksmanship.'

'I wonder what he is doing,' mused Sally.

'Waiting for me to come back, I suppose. Artemus is rather helpless,'

'Helpless?' laughed Sally.

'Yes—he needs me.'

'Monty, have you any idea what a cowboy means when he says that a man is "forked" or "salty"?'

'No, I haven't any idea.'

'Well, it is their idea of a *man,* Monty. It means that they can hold their own in a country like this.'

'Hm-m-m-m. That is interesting. By Jove, he may be doing something to help us out. I'm glad to hear about him. But I would much rather have Hashknife Hartley and Sleepy looking for us.'

'I guess we will just have to wait, Monty. It doesn't seem to be a very bright outlook—but anything can happen, especially in Arizona.'

'You would say that, Sally—you're wonderful.'

'I'm not wonderful. I'm tired and hungry and I'd like to cry—but what is the use? I wonder if they really sent a letter to your father, asking him for money.'

'I wonder.'

'Would he send it, Monty?'

'I don't know. He is a cold-blooded, deliberate man, Sally. They say on Wall Street that he always gets value received on every deal. He would never understand the gravity of my position until a complete investigation had been made. He might think it a hoax—and that I was at the bottom of it. I'm afraid we must eliminate Dad as a factor in this; he is too far away. I'm sorry, Sally.'

'It's all right, Monty. He might as well keep his money, because I don't believe they would turn us loose, even if they got the money.'

'Do you believe it is that bad for us, Sally?'

'I do. If your knowledge of a left-handed man got us into this—why would they ever turn us loose?'

'I—I wish I hadn't been in that bank,' he said wearily.

'We'll see what happens in the morning,' said Sally. 'At least, we are free—now.'

About an hour later a man on a jaded horse came down the canyon trail. He dismounted at the shack, hammered on the door but got no answer, so he went inside and lighted a candle. It was Panamint, the cook from the Circle JR. He looked with amazement at the trussed-up Sody, and then cut him loose. Sody was mad, as he massaged his cramped lips and jaws.

'What're you doin' here, Panamint?' he whispered.

'That damn sheriff and deputy,' said Panamint huskily. 'I was takin' Jack Rett's body back to the ranch when I met 'em. I—I didn't think up a good lie; so I high-tailed it through the brush, leavin' the horse and body. Since then'—Panamint stopped to catch his breath—'since then, I've been dodgin' 'em. But who the hell tied you up?'

'Hashknife Hartley and his gang,' whispered Sody. 'They're here—in the canyon—three of 'em. We've got to git out, Panamint.'

Sody got up and leaned against the bunk. Panamint's eyes flashed to the half-open door.

'Hartley, eh? Maybe we can trap 'em, Sody.'

'Don't be a damn fool, Panamint; I tried that. They hit me with a can of beans and knocked me down.'

'Are you crazy?'

'I—I think so. I 'member 'em tellin' me that they knocked out Tex and Slim and tied 'em up at the top of the trail.'

'Mebbe yuh didn't dream it—there wasn't a guard at the top. Here's my extra gun. You stand guard down here—I'll find out about Tex and Slim.'

Sody's hand shook as he took the gun.

'They whopped yuh in the eye, eh?' remarked Panamint.

'The dude done that. He got a hand loose. Up here's where the can of beans hit me. Cut m' head, too.'

Panamint went over to the doorway and looked out, listening intently. Then he said: 'I'll find out about the boys. If anybody shows up—start shootin'.'

'I've been learned,' said Sody painfully.

He shut the door and sat down on the bunk in the flickering candlelight, the gun clenched in

230

his right hand. Sody had little imagination, but he realized the gravity of the situation. Jack Rett dead, Slim and Tex tied up, possibly injured, Hashknife Hartley and his two men somewhere in the canyon, and the sheriff and deputy, very likely, still trying to find the trail into the canyon.

'If they git me, I'm a goner—sure,' breathed Sody. 'Damn that dude! I knowed it wasn't a good scheme. The rest of 'em, in and out, havin' a chance to keep their damn skins—and me, hived up here—'

Sody stiffened. He heard brush breaking outside. He drew back the hammer on his gun, every muscle tensed.

The door was flung open and a man sprang in. The candle flickered so badly that the illumination was almost nil, but Sody pulled the trigger, and the man went sprawling against the opposite wall. Slowly Sody got off the bunk, coughing a little in the acrid smoke.

'Panamint!' he said huskily. 'Damn you, Panamint, why did yuh—'

'You shot me!' husked Panamint. 'You . . . fool! The . . . sheriff . . . is . . . comin' . . . down . . . the . . . trail. I . . . I . . . you . . . fool . . .'

Panamint sprawled against the wall, his voice stilled. Sody stared wide-eyed into space. He had killed Panamint. That was funny. He didn't expect him back so soon.

He said, 'You danged fool, why didn't yuh knock?'

But Panamint didn't answer. Sody leaned against the wall, breathing heavily. Trapped! The sheriff coming down the trail! Sody's eyes turned toward the bunk. Dynamite! Of course! If he had time—

He acted swiftly. The cover was loose on the box, and he worked feverishly to pour the yellow sticks into a gunnysack. A full box of detonating caps and a coil of fuse went into the sack.

'Them holes have been bored for a year,' he muttered. 'Damn 'em, I can seal up this canyon so damn tight that nothin' but a buzzard can ever get out.'

He swung the sack over his shoulder and went to the doorway, where he listened for several moments. Then he slipped out into the darkness and began crawling through the brush in the general direction of the trail. Finally he stopped and flattened on the ground.

'Got to wait for daylight,' he muttered. 'Trail too dangerous, and I can't find the holes in the dark.'

Hashknife, Sleepy, and Artemus were having a hard time in the darkness. There did not seem to be any trails. Artemus wanted to go back and get another can of beans.

'I've just got m' appetite back,' he declared. 'How 'bout you, Sleepy?'

'Forget food,' advised Hashknife. 'Somewhere in this hole are the dude and Sally Harder. We've got to find them.'

'I wouldn't know either of 'em in this darkness, even if I was standin' right on 'em,' sighed Artemus. 'I wonder which way is that shack.'

'Never mind the shack,' said Hashknife. 'We're stayin' right here until mornin'. Make yourselves comfortable.'

'And I can't even go back for more beans?' asked Artemus.

'You couldn't find that shack with a lantern.'

'I've got a darn good nose,' said Artemus. 'Say, how would it be if we yelled for them lost folks?'

'No yellin',' replied Hashknife. 'We'll start searchin' at daylight.'

'Mebbe they've already fell into a hole,' said Artemus.

'You have beautiful thoughts,' said Sleepy.

'That's plain hunger. I'd feel different if I had more beans.'

Later they heard the shot that killed Panamint, but had no idea where it had been fired. Far up on the opposite rim of the canyon a coyote wailed mournfully. It was cold down there among the rocks and brush as they huddled together, waiting for the first streak of daylight.

Gradually things began to take shape. Daylight would be later deep in the canyon than on the rim. Hashknife watched the cliffs near the rim, and as soon as he could see them in vague detail, he spoke to the others and they got to their feet, stiff and tired.

'This a terrible big canyon,' said Artemus. 'Yuh could hide a herd of dinny-sours in here and never find 'em in a month of Sundays.'

Hashknife led the search. He had a sort of an idea where the cabin was located, and he knew they were not very far from it. That shot might indicate that some of the gang were still in the canyon, and there was danger of an ambush.

After fifteen or twenty minutes of worming through the canyon, they ran into several head of range cattle, branded with both the Quarter-Circle H and the Rocking R.

'They bring 'em in here in small bunches and alter the brands,' said Hashknife, 'and then they send 'em on to the Circle JR.'

'Smart,' remarked Artemus. 'Smart as hell.'

'Yeah,' said Sleepy dryly. 'Very smart.'

'Until they started mixin' murder with rustlin',' said Hashknife. 'Come here, Artemus. I'll boost yuh up on top of this rock, and yuh can climb to the top of the pile. Maybe you can see somethin' from there.'

'I'm sure good at lookin',' grinned Artemus. 'I might see a restaurant.'

Dawn found Sally and Montgomery sore and stiff. They, too, had heard the one shot fired, but had no idea where it had been fired. They had enjoyed little sleep.

'I'm a sight,' said Sally wearily.

'The one sight in the world that I want to see,' said Montgomery.

They looked at each other and tried to laugh, but it was only a grimace. Montgomery rubbed his stubbled jaws and looked with weary eyes at the piles of brush-grown rocks. Suddenly he blinked. On the top of a high pile of rocks he had seen a man, and the top of those rocks was not over a hundred feet away.

He picked up his revolver, his eyes on the rocks. Sally saw the expression on his face and followed his gaze. There *was* a man there and he stood up in plain view, looking around.

Alexander Hamilton Montgomery had a vague idea of marksmanship. He lifted the big gun in both hands, took an erratic aim, and pulled the trigger. The heavy report blasted back from the sides of the canyon, and the man on the rocks seemed to jump straight up and sail off into the brush.

Alexander Hamilton Montgomery dropped the gun and yelled at the top of his voice, 'Artemus! Artemus Day!'

'Have you lost your mind?' asked Sally nervously.

'That was Artemus!' choked Montgomery. 'Didn't you see his legs?'

'His legs?'

'Yes, when he jumped. He has the only pair like that on earth.'

Then he yelled for Artemus again, and the voice echoed back and forth along the rocky walls, as though a dozen voices were yelling for Artemus.

In about two minutes Artemus called, 'Is that you, Mr. Montgomery?'

'Yes—come quick!' replied Montgomery.

In another minute or two, Hashknife, Sleepy, and Artemus came squirming through the brush.

'Yo're all right?' asked Hashknife anxiously.

'We're all right,' laughed Sally. 'Don't we look it?'

'How did you find us, Artemus?' asked Montgomery.

'Just a moment,' interrupted Hashknife. 'This is no time to tell our life-history. Do you know which way to that shack?'

'Back that way,' said Sally, pointing.

Hashknife nodded. 'That's what I thought. Come on, and go carefully, because we don't know what's ahead of us. Somebody fired a shot last night over at the shack, I think.'

'We heard it,' said Sally. 'Do you think we can get out of here?'

'That is in the laps of the gods, Miss Sally. Keep as low as possible, because yuh never can tell where a dry-gulcher might be planted.'

'Have you seen my father lately?' she asked.

'Not lately. No more talkin'—please.'

Jim Martin, the sheriff, and Mañana Higgins found the trail into the canyon, and they found their way down to the hidden shack. They heard the shot that killed Panamint, but they did not know who fired it. In fact, they didn't know Panamint. They examined the cabin, found the cut ropes, and did a lot of wondering what had happened there.

'It's sure got me beat,' declared the sheriff. 'I never knew there was a trail into this canyon before. Who is this feller—and who shot him?'

'Anyway,' said Mañana, 'this canyon is out of our county, Jim.'

'I can still wonder, can't I?'

'Uh-huh. As far as that goes, who killed Jack Rett? And what's the Circle JR doin' over here? Hell, this is miles off their range, Jim. And where's Hashknife and Sleepy and Smoky Day?'

'*Quien sabe?*' replied the sheriff. He picked up the candle and examined the floor near the bunk.

'What's all this fresh sawdust on the floor, Mañana?'

'I dunno. I noticed it awhile ago. Wait a minute! That's sawdust out of a dynamite box. There's the box, two-thirds empty.'

'Dynamite? Who'd be usin' dynamite here. Why—that's funny.'

'Funny—yeah,' agreed the sheriff. 'I don't like this layout. Mañana, you go to the top of the trail, while I watch down here. If anybody tries to come in here—stop 'em.'

Mañana hurried away to the trail, and Jim Martin sat down against the shack, trying to puzzle out the reason for the shack in the brush and a dead man in the shack.

Finally he went back into the shack and searched the dead man, whose pockets produced a few dollars, a knife, and some old keys. Deep in a hip-pocket of his overalls was a folded envelope, addressed to Jack Rett, Turquoise Springs, Arizona. The letter, scrawled with soft pencil, was smudged, but decipherable. It read:

> Got to lay low. Things bad here. You better mark that bunch and get them out safe and quick. Will let you know about things later.

And the letter was signed by the one initial M. Jim Martin pondered over the letter by candlelight. The letter was postmarked Antelope Flats. Someone in Antelope Flats had to lay low. The sheriff knew that to 'mark the bunch' meant to brand some stock. He knew now that Jack Rett was a rustler, working in conjunction with someone in Lost Horse Valley. But who killed Jack Rett? Some of his own gang?

The man on the floor could have answered those questions, but he was not answering any more questions. After a while Jim Martin went to the doorway. Daylight was coming. He went away from the shack and hunkered down in the brush. In that way he could watch the cabin and not be trapped by anyone. Not over a hundred feet away, hidden in the brush, was Sody. He knew that one of the two men had gone up the trail. Panamint had said that they were the sheriff and deputy.

Gradually the canyon lighted. Jim Martin relaxed. He was tired from continual riding and loss of sleep. He and Mañana had gone to the Circle JR ranch, but found the place deserted. That fact had seemed queer; but they came back, only to meet a man on a horse, leading another horse, on which was the body of Jack Rett. The man got away, but they trailed him back to the close vicinity of the canyon.

Suddenly a shot rang out, not far away. Jim Martin was on the alert. Shortly after the shot was fired, he heard sounds, very much as though someone was yelling loudly. The multiple echoes made it confusing.

Jim Martin was not tired or sleepy now. If anyone came to that shack, he was going to make things uncomfortable for him. After a while he saw a moving object in the brush. It was only a flash. He kept watching the shack, and

239

in a few moments a man, traveling with all the stealth of an Indian, came along close to the wall of the shack. He eased in against the corner and looked around at the half-open doorway.

'Hartley!' he said sharply.

Hashknife slowly turned his head and looked toward the sound of the voice.

'Hyah, Sheriff,' he said quietly. Then he turned and whistled the call of the mocker, paying no more attention to the sheriff, who came from the brush, gun in hand. In a few moments Sally, Montgomery, Sleepy, and Artemus filed out of the brush. Jim Martin looked at them in amazement, as they all came around to the front of the shack.

Sody could see them too, and began backing away, dragging his sack.

'Damn yuh,' he snarled to himself. 'I'll bury yuh down here if it's the last thing I ever do. One man up the trail, but I'll stop him. Give me about five minutes' start, and you'll never get out.'

Jim Martin stared at Sally and Montgomery for several moments, and turned to Hashknife.

'How did you ever find 'em?' he asked huskily.

'The story's too long,' replied Hashknife. 'When we're out of this canyon, I'll tell yuh all I know.'

'Who's the dead man in the shack?' asked the sheriff.

'Dead man? Oh, yeah—that shot in the night.'

Hashknife and Sleepy went in with Jim Martin.

'That's Panamint,' said Hashknife. 'The cook at the Circle JR. Martin, this is where they mis-branded Quarter-Circle H and Rockin' R cattle, and made 'em Circle JR.'

'By gad, that works out!' exploded the sheriff. 'I got a letter from this man's pocket . . . what's the matter, Hartley?'

'That sawdust!' exclaimed Hashknife. 'Look! That box of dynamite is nearly empty! Get out of this cabin—quick! It might be . . . scatter around out there . . . I'll be back!'

And while they stood looking in amazement, Hashknife was running swiftly through the brushy trail, heading for the trail up the wall of the canyon.

'What in hell bit him?' gasped the sheriff.

'Search me,' replied Sleepy foolishly. 'He's scared, I tell yuh.'

'Scared?' queried the sheriff.

'I didn't mean it that way.'

'It was that dynamite,' said the sheriff. 'Mebbe he's got an idea that somethin' is wrong. I wonder—'

'That's right!' blurted Sleepy. 'That box was full last night. Maybe they're goin' to dynamite the trail!'

Hashknife had the same idea. Men as desperate as those would have some way of frustrating an attack. He was running up the steep trail, stumbling along, trying to prevent anyone from

241

burying them in that canyon. It was hard work, and his already tired legs almost refused. Up and up he went. He had never seen the trail before. It twisted and turned, dug fairly deep in the canyon wall.

Then it came up along the face of a sheer cliff and made an abrupt left-hand turn on solid rock. Hashknife's lungs were aching from the strain, and his eyes were full of perspiration, when he saw the crouching figure against the inside wall of the trail.

It was Sody, working feverishly to fill a hole with sticks of dynamite. Hashknife stopped twenty feet away, but Sody didn't hear him, nor see him, because his back was down the trail.

'Don't move, Sody!' gasped Hashknife. 'Yo're through, Sody!'

He saw Sody's shoulders move convulsively, but the man said nothing.

'Get to yore feet, Sody,' ordered Hashknife. 'One move, and I'll shoot yuh. This is Hartley.'

Sody did not turn his head, and Hashknife could not see his hands.

'You'll never take me, Hartley,' said Sody. 'There ain't no rope long enough to ever hang me.'

'Rope or bullet, Sody—they both kill.'

The sack of dynamite was near Sody's right foot, and on top of the sack was the box of detonators. And before Hashknife had any idea of Sody's intentions, he drew his gun and fired it squarely into the box of detonators.

Hashknife was knocked flat on the trail by the explosion, which fairly shook the side of the hill. Rocks rained down, and slides of loose rubble came falling, almost burying Hashknife. He had several cuts on his head and face, but was more dazed than hurt.

Of Sody, there was no trace. Nor did his blast injure the trail. The rock was too hard for that unconfined dynamite to do more than crack it, and a few chunks sloughed off into the canyon. Hashknife examined the spot. He could see the drilled holes, where Sody had planned to blow away a huge section of the rocky trail, making an exit impossible. There was no way around. The Lost Horse Gang had planned well.

Slowly Hashknife went down the trail. The others were coming to meet him, and they went up together, while Hashknife told the story.

'He deliberately blew himself up?' asked the sheriff in amazement.

'He didn't like ropes,' replied Hashknife. 'I don't blame him.'

'What are you carryin', Smoky?' asked the sheriff.

'Seven cans of beans,' replied Artemus. 'I went back and got 'em. It was all they had left.'

It was a hard climb to the rim of the canyon,

where they stopped for a brief rest at the head of the trail.

'You prob'ly got a lot to put in yore play,' said Artemus.

'Too much for a play,' said Montgomery wearily. 'They were going to kill both of us— Sally and me. Now they're dead—and we are alive. Life is queer, isn't it? Hashknife, I believe it is just as you said about that Big Book; our names are still clear.'

'You never know yore luck,' replied Hashknife soberly.

'Luck—hell!' snorted Artemus. 'It wasn't luck that made Hashknife look into that darned canyon. He came straight here to the trail, when nobody in Antelope Flats, except them crooks, knowed there was a trail to the bottom. It wasn't luck that sent him to the Circle JR. Don't talk to me about luck.'

'It wasn't luck,' agreed the sheriff. 'I had a hunch they had gone to the Circle JR. And it wasn't luck that sent Hartley up this trail, tryin' to head off that trail-blastin' Sody. We can get those cows out—and the rustlin' is over, I hope.'

'It will be good to be home,' said Sally. 'The whole thing seems like a nightmare.'

A pair of buzzards slanted down toward the bottom of the canyon, and Sally shuddered as she pointed at them.

'They would have come after us like that,' she said simply.

'I reckon we better start home,' said Hashknife. 'It's a long ride.'

'Well, we won't starve,' said Artemus. 'I've got seven cans of beans.'

CHAPTER XVI

GUN SMOKE IN THE PRONG HORN SALOON

THE town of Antelope Flats was in a state of suspense. Volunteer searchers combed the Valley, while the people in the town ignored business, waiting and watching for some word, wondering what had become of Hashknife, Sleepy, Artemus, together with the sheriff and deputy. They argued that some of them should be back soon.

Flint Harder came to town early each morning and spent the day, and far into the evening, sitting in his buckboard in front of the hotel. He did not curse anyone now. He saw Nell and Mrs. Long come to the jail to talk with Danny Long. Alphabet Anderson was acting as jailer. Swede Olson sat around the livery-stable, drinking gin with Anderson and Joe Le Blanc, the blacksmith. There was nothing else to do.

A telegram came for the sheriff, and Alphabet opened it. The message was from Alexander Hamilton Montgomery's father, and read:

WIRE MORE DETAILS. WILLING TO PAY THE MONEY UNLESS THIS IS A HOAX.

'What's a hoax?' asked Alphabet. He pronounced it 'ho-ax.'

'Das is a grubbin' hoe,' said Swede. 'Yust like pickaxe.'

Swede took the telegram and examined it.

'Yames A. Montgomery,' he read. 'Maybe das sheriff is buying a hoe-axe from Montgomery Vard.'

'Sure,' agreed Alphabet. 'You are smart man, Svede.'

'Ay am damn fool,' gloomed Swede. 'Pass de yin, Yoe.'

'By gar this telegram sound like those sheriff is try for sell hoe-axe to Mr. Montgomery,' said Joe Le Blanc. 'He say he pay the money if this is *not* hoe-axe.'

'Oh, he don't want one, eh?' queried Alphabet. 'Vell, can you beat that? He don't know a hoe-axe ven he sees von. Svede, you are drunk.'

'Yah, su-ure,' admitted Swede.

Mrs. Harder and Mrs. Long came from the jail, after their talk with Danny. Alphabet Anderson let them have the run of the place. After all, he was only jailer, *pro-tem.* They came up the street, going to the post-office, and had to pass the Quarter-Circle H buckboard.

Nell Harder stopped and looked at Flint, and for several moments they looked at each other. Mrs. Long went on a few steps, but stopped.

Nell said, 'No news, Mr. Harder?'

248

He shook his head slowly. It was the first time she had spoken to him since long before she and Dean had been married.

Mrs. Long said, 'I'll go to the post-office, Nell,' and went along.

Flint Harder looked at Mrs. Long, as she went up the street, and then turned to Nell. 'Come over here,' he said huskily.

She came over beside the buckboard and he slid painfully over to the other side of the seat. Then she climbed up on the seat. Neither of them spoke for a long time.

Finally she said, 'Did you send me some money?'

'What made you think that?' he asked.

'I got three letters,' she replied quietly. 'The envelopes had all been addressed by the same man. One contained two hundred, one contained five hundred, and the last one one hundred dollars.'

Flint Harder scowled thoughtfully. 'You got *three* letters, Nell?'

'Yes.'

'Well, I—I don't know . . . we won't worry about them.'

'There won't be anything to worry about—if Sally comes back,' she said.

'No,' he said, 'there won't be anything to worry about. You'll come out and live with us, Nell. I've thought a lot about things—lately.

I'm not half as big as I thought I was. I've always known that I was a fool. I wanted to hate everybody. I didn't want any friends. You know that.'

'Dean always said you wasn't like people thought you were.'

'He did? Nell, you're not sayin' that, just because—'

'No, I'm not.'

'God, what a fool I was! That day he came out and asked me for money, and I laughed at him. A hundred dollars. I laughed at him—and see what he done. I drove him to it, Nell—my own son. Don't shake yore head—I know. I've had time to realize. I guess it was Hartley, that tall cowboy. He knows more what was in my heart than I did. He made me sit down and think. I hope he comes back, so I can thank him.'

'You're not the same,' she said quietly, 'and I'm glad. I don't want anybody to hate me.'

'I didn't hate you. I didn't hate Dean. And, by God, I don't hate Jim Martin! Do you hear that? I hated myself—and I thought I hated all of you. My soul was warped. Hartley told me what was wrong with me.'

'I'm glad you don't hate Dad,' she said simply. 'I've had time to think things over—since Dean died. Dad was not to blame. Mr. Hartley told me that it was Fate—not my father. Life is like that, he says.'

'I know, Nell,' he said gently. 'We've got to go on, doin' the best we can. I don't believe I've got a friend on earth. I realize that—now. But maybe I can get some of them back. If I can't—it's my fault. But tomorrow I'll send the boys over and move your stuff to the ranch. You'll come, won't you, Nell?'

'Yes, I'll come,' she said quietly.

'I wonder if Mrs. Long would come too, Nell. She's alone. I'll do what I can to help Danny. I can get him a good lawyer. I believe a good one can tear hell out of Swede's testimony.'

Suddenly his eyes clouded and he shook his head.

'I almost forgot Sally,' he said huskily. 'Why don't some of them come back? It's hell—sitting here—watching.'

Andy Vincent, the elderly proprietor of the hotel, came to the doorway, spat dryly, and walked back.

'Anythin',' he told the four walls, 'can happen, if yuh wait long enough, but I never expected to live long enough to see them two settin' on a buckboard seat together.'

A number of riders came into town, dusty and weary. Nick Higby and Pete Soboba were among them. They came past the buckboard, staring at Flint Harder and Nell. Higby shook his head at Flint Harder, indicating that there was no news. Mike Lassen and Ed North, the left-handed

251

cowboy from the Rocking R, rode in and tied their horses at the Prong Horn hitch-rack.

'For some reason,' said Nell, 'I have a feeling that Hashknife Hartley will come back with news. Dad and Mañana are somewhere—'

'Yeah,' said Flint Harder absently. 'There's five of 'em—Hartley, Stevens, Jim Martin, Mañana Higgins—and that damn bowlegged pest— Smoky Day. I—I want him to come back—for just one reason.'

'What reason is that?' asked Nell.

'I want to ask that little bowlegged devil who he addressed those other two envelopes for.'

It was about eight o'clock that evening when the caravan came in behind the hotel. Slim Sherrod and Tex McCall were together on one horse, and they were quickly placed in jail. Then the rest of them came into the hotel from the rear. Andy Vincent gasped and almost fell off his stool behind the counter when he saw all the missing persons.

'Your father—out there in the buckboard!' he exclaimed, pointing. 'He's been there every day—all day, Sally.'

She went out to him, while Hashknife, Sleepy, Jim Martin, and Mañana conferred quietly. Then they went out, followed by Artemus Day, and crossed the street, ignoring the two people in the buckboard.

The hitch-rack at the saloon was full of horses,

and there was a crowd in the saloon. At the bar, among the others, were Nick Higby, Pete Soboba, from the Quarter-Circle H, and Mike Lassen and Ed North, from the Rocking R. Bob Reynolds, owner of the Rocking R, was also at the bar. The air was foggy with tobacco smoke as the men came in.

Somebody said: 'Here they are! Now we'll know somethin'!'

Hashknife was in the lead, a tall, gaunt, dusty-faced figure. Behind him came Sleepy, who moved to the right and stopped against a card table. Jim Martin, the sheriff, and Mañana went on a little farther. The faces of all four men were grim and determined. Artemus stopped near the front doorway.

Nick Higby, backed against the bar, a drink in his left hand, his left heel hooked over the bar rail, said, 'Well, what luck, Hartley?'

Hashknife was looking straight at him, as he said quietly: 'All the luck in the world, Higby. Sally Harder is with her father, and the dude is at the hotel.'

A flash of fright showed in Higby's eyes. Soboba moved around slowly, and both Mike Lassen and Ed North shifted positions.

'You—uh—found them, Hartley?' queried Higby, his voice faltering.

'We found 'em, Higby. Before Jack Rett died, he sent you this.'

Hashknife took a folded paper from his pocket and handed it to Nick Higby, who drew back.

'Jack Rett?' he said. 'Before he died? What do yuh mean? He wouldn't send me a letter. When did he die?'

'I'll read it to yuh,' offered Hashknife. 'He said you'd understand. But'—Hashknife smiled with his lips—'I forgot the money he sent. Here it is—nine hundred and sixty dollars, Higby. The note reads: "Ninety-six head of cows at twenty a head, nineteen hundred and twenty dollars. One half for your gang, nine hundred and sixty dollars."'

'What in hell was that?' exploded Bob Reynolds.

'A little transaction in cows,' replied Hashknife slowly. 'They had to sell 'em cheap, Mr. Reynolds—because they stole 'em. The Circle JR sold 'em and gave half to Higby and his gang.'

'My cattle?' queried Reynolds, in amazement.

'Half-and-half, I reckon,' replied Hashknife. 'Half yours and half belonged to Flint Harder.'

Nick Higby licked his dry lips, as he looked at the money in his hand. The saloon was deathly quiet now. Suddenly he flung the money on the floor.

'Damn yuh, that ain't my money!' he exclaimed huskily. 'You can't hang nothin' on me, Hartley. Yo're bluffin' and you know it.'

Hashknife's lips smiled, but his eyes never

254

changed, as he slowly shifted and looked at Lassen, whose jaw tightened. He was in a tight spot, and he knew it.

'Then it belongs to Mike Lassen,' said Hashknife. 'By the way, Lassen, when Panamint died he had a letter you wrote to Jack Rett. It makes good readin', too. Have you got the nerve to stand there and let me read it out loud to the folks?'

'No—I never wrote—I don't even know Jack Rett,' denied Lassen.

Hashknife laughed quietly. 'Not even a good bluffer, Lassen,' he said. 'I remember the night the Texas Rangers caught you—'

'It's a lie!' rasped Lassen. 'They never caught me—I—what the hell are you talkin' about?'

'You,' replied Hashknife evenly. 'And the day of the bank robbery, Lassen. You and Nick Higby got away, with Lon Porter ridin' between yuh. One of the sheriff's bullets hit Lon. He was dyin'. You met Dean Harder, and you had to kill him to save yore own skins, so yuh shot him, Lassen.'

Lassen was staring at Hashknife, his eyes mere pinpoints, his lips drawn to a penciled line.

'You left Dean there, Lassen,' continued Hashknife, in a deadly cold voice. 'You knew he'd be blamed for bein' the third man—and then yuh planted Lon Porter in Danny Long's stable. You had to get rid of the body. You shot Dean in the back, Lassen.'

'That's a lie!' screamed Lassen. 'It was Nick Higby, and—'

The action was almost too fast to follow. They were trapped; trapped by Mike Lassen's statement. Guns thundered in the Prong Horn Saloon; eight guns to be exact, but four of them were faster. Mike Lassen and Ed North were down, flat on the floor.

Pete Soboba went staggering into a card table, his finger still pulling the trigger of his gun, but the bullets were smashing into the floor. Nick Higby, shocked by two forty-fives, still clung to the bar, but his gun was on the floor. It was all over in split seconds. Not a man spoke. Somebody coughed in the smoke, and a man blew the smoke away from his face with a wave of his hand. Higby's eyes were closed, and he was using every effort to keep upright.

From the doorway came Artemus's voice. 'Now, I hope we can go and eat.'

It seemed to break the spell. Nick Higby's knees collapsed and he went sprawling. Pete Soboba, on his hands and knees, blubbered: 'We made a mistake. Rustlin' was all right . . . but murder and kidnappin' . . . wasn't . . . in . . . our . . . line . . .'

Jim Martin came over to Hashknife and held out his hand.

'You had the right idea, Hartley,' he said. 'You said they'd convict themselves.'

'Give a calf enough rope . . .' said Hashknife wearily.

The room was in an uproar. Men ran to get the doctor, others ran to see Sally Harder. Hashknife and Sleepy, half-starved, went outside. Artemus was doing a bowlegged dance on the saloon porch.

'Workin' up m' appetite,' he said dryly. 'How soon do we eat?'

Men were surging around them. Flint Harder, relying very little on his cane, was trying to shake hands with Hashknife, while the rest of Antelope Flats was trying to do the same thing.

'My son didn't do it!' blurted Flint Harder. 'He never robbed any bank!'

'Yumpin' Yudas!' howled Swede Olson. 'Danny never shoot him!'

'Danny Long's free!' yelped another.

Hashknife smiled down at Flint Harder. Sally and Alexander Hamilton Montgomery joined them.

'It's all right,' said Flint Harder. 'Nell is goin' to live with us, and Sally is goin' to marry this damn dude. How do yuh like that?'

'How do you like it?' countered Hashknife.

'I like it!'

'That's all that's needed,' said Hashknife quietly.

Jim Martin released Danny Long, and they came together. Hashknife smiled slowly and said,

'Flint Harder, I'd like to have yuh shake hands with Jim Martin.'

They looked at each other for a moment, and their hands met. Artemus chuckled.

Flint Harder said: 'Smoky, who sent those other amounts of money to Nell? You wrote the envelopes.'

'I sent one,' said Jim Martin. 'Mine was for a hundred.'

'Mine was for two hundred,' said Alexander Hamilton Montgomery. 'Was I wrong in doing it?'

'Son,' said Hashknife quietly, 'you were just right.'

They slipped away from the crowd and went down to the little depot, where they hammered on the door until the agent came down from his living-quarters.

'Any news about the missin' people?' he asked.

'Is there somebody missin'?' asked Sleepy innocently.

'There either is, or I've been lied to.'

'Everybody accounted for.'

Hashknife wrote a telegram to Bob Marsh. It read:

HENRY WEBSTER RESPONSIBLE
FOR DEMISE OF LOST HORSE GANG.
SLEEPY SENDS HIS REGARDS.

As they turned away, after paying for the telegram, Alexander Hamilton Montgomery came in.

'I better wire my father,' he said. 'He might be worrying.'

'He prob'ly don't know yuh very well,' said Sleepy.

The young man wired:

AM SAFE AND WELL BUT COULD USE THE TWENTY THOUSAND DOLLARS AS I AM GETTING MARRIED. I AM NOT GOING TO WRITE A PLAY OF THE WEST BUT I AM GOING TO LIVE IT. SALLY SAYS I'M AS FORKED AS A MESQUITE AND AS SALTY AS THE SEA. LETTER FOLLOWS.

'Sally must like you,' said Hashknife.

'Why, yes, I believe she does. She says that anything can happen in Arizona—and I believe it has.'

'Yeah,' said Hashknife dryly. 'I reckon she's right—it has.'

An hour later, two dim figures rode through the starlight, heading out of Lost Horse Valley. Their job was over.

'It's a real nice place—this valley,' said Sleepy quietly.

'Yeah,' agreed Hashknife, 'but it's goin' to be

peaceful for a while, until somebody feels that he can cheat the law.'

'Uh-huh. Yuh know, pardner, about halfway between here and Isabella there's some tall hills off to the east. I saw 'em as we came in.'

'High ones—and kinda blue,' said Hashknife. 'Yuh never can tell what yuh might find on the other side.'

And there was only the jingle of bit-chains and the soft *plop, plop* of hoofs in the dusty road, as they went on in the darkness.

Books are produced in the United States using U.S.-based materials	Books are printed using a revolutionary new process called THINKtech™ that lowers energy usage by 70% and increases overall quality	Books are durable and flexible because of Smyth-sewing	Paper is sourced using environmentally responsible foresting methods and the paper is acid-free

Center Point Large Print
600 Brooks Road / PO Box 1
Thorndike, ME 04986-0001 USA

(207) 568-3717

US & Canada:
1 800 929-9108
www.centerpointlargeprint.com